NO ONE CAN HIDE

Reuben Cole Westerns Book 4

STUART G YATES

For Janice,
hoping you enjoy this one as much as the others!

CHAPTER ONE

C atherine "Cathy" Courtauld lived on the far side of the river in a small log cabin her husband Jude built before he died of scarlet fever in the summer of 1870. Some people from the nearby town of Bethlehem believed he had picked up something awful from one of the many bordellos he was known to frequent, but Cathy did her best not to listen to such spurious, hurtful gossip. People were jealous of what she and her husband had achieved in such a short span of time, and when folk are jealous, they allow their tongues to wag. That was how she saw it, and nothing much had happened since to convince her otherwise. Jude was a good man, and she missed him. Well, "good" in the sense that he provided. She wasn't so certain about everything else.

A slim, strikingly handsome woman, she worked tirelessly to keep the family smallholding in good condition, something in which she excelled. Nevertheless, loneliness gnawed into her bones. The land was uncompromising, the soil hard, the weather lacking in rain. She longed for a partner to share her burdens.

The late afternoon she heard the spattering of gunfire, she

was on her knees, weeding through the root crop. She stopped, senses alerted. Cautiously, she raised her head and squinted towards the distant tree line. In one direction, the river formed a natural barrier for her land, another a cluster of trees, interspersed with bracken and shrub, another. It was from somewhere within this area that the gunfire came.

For a long moment, she considered running back to her cabin, to find the Henry carbine she always kept in her buggy. It hadn't been fired since Jude was alive, and she had no idea where extra cartridges were kept. So she squatted and waited and prayed that whoever it was wouldn't approach her place.

But they did.

Four men riding shaggy looking mares, their faces cast into deep shadow by the brims of their dusty hats. She flattened herself, putting her cheek against the earth. Perhaps if she remained deathly still, they wouldn't notice her.

They were close now, steering their mounts around the root crop field. She gave up a tiny prayer of thanks for that.

"We should go see who is in there."

"Could be they heard the gunfire."

"Could be they have seen us."

These three statements came from three distinctly different voices, one clearly Mexican, one old and gruff, the third much younger, a tinge of fear on the edge of his words. The fourth, when he spoke, was that of their obvious leader. A man well used to giving orders, of others doing as he bid. "If they had heard, we'd see 'em running, and I'd kill them dead before they opened their blabbering mouths."

"So who lives there, Jonas?"

"I don't know and I don't care. Maybe they is in town picking up supplies. I don't see no buggy."

This much was true. Cathy did possess a buggy, but it was stored away in the barn. When she needed to, she rode into town on her colt, Pharaoh. Pharaoh had thrown a shoe some days previously, and the blacksmith was due any day now. She sheltered in the small stable, together with her *burro* friend. Being out of sight proved another reason to thank God.

The riders moved on, the clomping of hooves gradually fading away until, ears straining to hear, Cathy caught the sound of water splashing. They were crossing the river and heading away from her place.

She let out a long sigh, rolled over onto her back, and settled herself before climbing to her feet. She gave a look around. Satisfied no one remained behind, she broke into a run. Not towards the house, however. Towards where the gunshots came.

In a dip amongst the trees where the harsh warmth of the sun could not penetrate, she found him.

Shot. Two times. Once in the left shoulder, once in the chest. He appeared to be dead, the pallor of his flesh waxen, drained of color. He was young, had been handsome, smooth-faced. They had taken his gun, his hat, his boots, leaving him to bleed out alone in this sad and dreary place. It was the blood that made her stop and take a closer look.

Dead don't bleed.

Quickly, she got down on her haunches and felt his neck for a pulse. A tiny gasp escaped from her throat.

He was alive.

She dressed his wounds as best she could, fetching water from her well, washing away the worst of it before wrapping bandages torn from the bedsheets she'd only recently purchased from the local town's merchandise store around him. He groaned several times, and she knew this was a good sign. When she put water to his lips, he coughed, and her heart leapt.

Returning to the smallholding at a run, she fetched

Brandy, the *burro*. Pharaoh didn't like that, but Cathy ignored her horse and led the donkey to the trees. There she fashioned a sort of sledge from fallen trees, threading them together in the way Jude had shown her to make wattle fencing. It took her a long time to struggle and place the wounded man on the sledge. Her grim determination saw her through, despite the weight of him. She paused several times to wipe the sweat from her brow but before long he was positioned on the sled and, satisfied, she led Brandy back to the cabin.

That night she lay him down by the fire as the fever came, the bullet in his chest the worst of the two. Bathing his brow, she watched him as he writhed around on the cabin floor. She thought he would die and dreaded the thought of having to dig a grave deep enough to deter coyotes. The hard earth would barely cover his body. But he did not die, and the morning dawned to find him breathing, an infection rattling in his chest. She washed away the sweat from his brow, changed the bandages covering his wounds, and made sure the fire was well stacked up.

She nursed him for another day before she accepted the inevitable – she would have to cut out the bullets if he were to survive.

He drifted in and out of consciousness, lucid moments few and far between. Managing to roll him onto an old piece of canvas, she sharpened one of her kitchen knives, held her breath, and worked on the lesser of the two wounds.

It proved a godsend he was unconscious for most of it.

The slug, when it came out, looked surprisingly small. She studied it for a long time, marveling how something so insignificant could cause such distress.

Setting to the second wound proved a far more laborious, stressful, and difficult task. It was in deep, forcing her to use a different knife with a thinner blade. At one point, he arched his back and bellowed, eyes snapping open, wild and afraid.

He tried to sit up, but she pushed him back down, put a wet cloth over his forehead, waited until his spasm subsided, then set to work once more.

It took something like twenty minutes to ease the bullet out, although it felt a lot longer. She was exhausted when she managed to lever it free.

The blood pulsed freely, but that had to be a good sign, and she packed the wound like the Kiowa had shown her all those years before, cleaning out the wound with some of Jude 's whisky before making a poultice from dampened, stale bread and herbs.

To her astonishment, as the evening wore on, his breathing grew lighter, the perspiration abated, and his almost constant moaning lessened until, finally, it ceased. He slept soundly. The following day, he sat up, face dry, eyes focused. She studied him from the far corner where she stood, the old Spencer in her hands. Who could guess what this man, now recovered, might try to do?

His lips, when he spoke, trembled slightly, his voice sounded raucous, the throat dry. "I could do with some water, ma'am, if you could be so kind."

Without any hesitation, she twisted around to where a goatskin gourd stood on the rickety table next to the water pump. She placed it on the floor within his arm's reach. Not for a single moment did her eyes leave his as she carefully stepped back.

He nodded his thanks, lifted the gourd to his lips, and drank fitfully, coughing hoarsely as the water hit his parched mouth.

"Take it slow," she said quietly.

Something passed across his eyes as he swallowed some more. A look of gratitude, so overwhelming that the tears came to his eyes and spilt down his cheeks. He looked away, ashamed at this show of emotion. 'I'm so very grateful for what you have done, ma'am.' He broke down and sobbed uncontrollably, head on his chest, shoulders heaving with the power of his outpourings.

Cathy watched, speechless, in two minds as to what to do. It could be a ploy, of course, to draw her to him, lower her guard so he could pounce, over-power her, and … and then what, she could only speculate. But something about the rawness of his tears made her think that this was no ruse. This was genuine, the sheer relief of being alive causing him to react in such an open, sincere way.

"I'm sorry," he said as the tears abated at last. He dabbed at his eyes with the back of his hand. Pulling a piece of white material from her sleeve, she crossed to him and pushed the makeshift handkerchief into his hand. He mopped at his wet face and smiled his thanks.

Stepping away again, Cathy studied him, the way his dark hair flopped over the left eye, the full, feminine mouth, smooth-cheeked, strong jawline not yet sprinkled with the shadow of a beard's growth. How old could he be? Eighteen? Twenty perhaps? And here he was, in her home, recovering from bullets which should have killed him. Who was he, and what had forced those others to attack him so viciously?

He caught her look, and his cheeks reddened slightly. "As soon as I'm able, I'll be on my way, ma'am. I don't wish to impose upon your hospitality any more than I need to."

"You're not imposing," she said, a slight smile playing across her mouth. "It was me that brought you in. And, besides, you can't go, not until you have some new boots."

He laughed, the relief palpable. "Ah, yes. They took those, I suppose." A sudden darkness came over his features. His eyes held hers. 'Did you see the men who did this to me?'

"No. Only heard them as they rode by."

"But they didn't see you?"

She frowned at the panic in his voice. "No. Don't worry yourself about that. I was on the ground, well hidden."

His shoulders visibly relaxed, and he lay back in the bed. "Thank you."

"Who were they? Why did they shoot you and leave you to die like that?"

She knew it was too soon to ask such searching questions. She had yet to gain his trust and, indeed, for him to gain hers. She held her breath, unable to take back her words, wondering if he would reveal it all or slip into coyness.

"We had a falling out," he said simply, his voice growing distant. "I'm sorry, ma'am. I'm tired. And I need ... you know ... I need ..."

"Yes!" she blurted, understanding immediately what he meant. "There is an outhouse round back. Are you sure you can walk?"

"If you were to put that carbine away, you could help me. At least to the door of the privy?" He sat up, laughing, and the sound cut through the tension which had settled between them.

"We'll see," she said, propped the carbine against the wall, and drew back her threadbare cardigan to reveal the Colt Navy stuffed into her skirt waistband. "My husband's. He taught me how to shoot, saying I'd need to if ever he was away on business and I was left alone."

"Is he away on business now?"

"Kind of." She took a step towards him. "Let's get you feeling a little more comfortable." She smiled and put out her hand. He took it after a moment's hesitation and slipped out from beneath the covers.

CHAPTER TWO

"I'll swear in a posse and run them down before sundown." Roose worked fresh cartridges into the Henry. He was breathing hard, his anger clear for all to see.

People began to gather around, staring at the bodies, muttering among themselves, commenting on how awful it all was, that such a lovely day could have ended in such a murderous way.

"We need to get these bodies off the street and go check the bank first," said Cole. "Put two armed men outside while we go inside."

Singling out two young men, both wearing tied down guns at their hips, Roose pointed to the bank. "Anyone but us comes out, you shoot 'em."

Appalled, the two young men exchanged nervous glances. Cole chuckled, "Don't worry, boys, I very much doubt there are any desperados left inside."

"Even so," muttered Roose.

"Even so, you just do what you can." Flashing them a wink, Cole inched forwards, alert, carbine ready. Roose scooted past, slamming himself against the wall adjacent to the entrance. He carefully propped the Henry beside him and drew his Colt Cavalry. Nodding to Cole, he eased back the hammer.

Cole went inside, sweeping the room with his Winchester. The three tellers behind the counter had their arms stretched upwards with such strain it looked like they were in pain. Cole pressed a single finger to his lips, gesturing with the Winchester for them to lower their hands. He scanned the rest of the room and, satisfied, lay down his carbine and pulled out his revolver. One of the tellers slowly pulled up the hatch to allow him to slip behind the counter. Cole went to the bank manager's office.

The door was part-open, and, using his foot, he pushed it wide, his gun ready.

There was paper money all over the floor, a lot of it splattered with fresh blood. Against the far wall, a man, clearly dead with his open eyes staring into space, a look of abject bewilderment etched across his frozen face.

A trail of more blood led to the rear entrance, usually heavily bolted with two thick iron bars giving further security. Everything was hanging open, the locks released by one of the keys from a bunch thrown onto the floor.

"He used my keys," explained a well-dressed and badly beaten man slumped in the corner, his mouth so swollen his words were barely recognizable.

Lowering himself to one knee, Cole peered through the crack in-between the door and the jam.

"The other one shot him."

Cole arched a single eyebrow and gave him a questioning glance.

"Young fella, very tall. He shot the both of them. They wanted to kill me, but he stopped them." He tried to sit upright but failed and, letting out a long wail of pain, slumped back down. "He saved my life."

"But only wounded the one who got away."

"Yes. Perhaps he was hoping you'd arrest him, throw him in jail."

"Why do that when there would be a chance he'd tell us everything he knows about the gang – their hideout, who they are, where they planned on headin'?"

"Who knows? Mister Cole, could you please send for a doctor? I'm not sure how much more of this pain I can take."

Returning his Colt to its holster, Cole stood and headed outside, picking up his carbine before gesturing the tellers to follow close behind.

"Anything?" asked Roose, visibly relaxing as Cole stepped up beside him.

"One dead, shot by one of his own according to the bank manager, who needs a doctor by the way. The other one he shot managed to get away. He'll be riding hell-for-leather to meet up with the rest of 'em." He nodded to the two young would-be gunslingers. "Thanks, boys, we won't be needing you today."

Looking relieved, they slinked away and headed towards the nearest saloon.

Roose watched them move away, then said, "Do we know which one did the shootin'?"

Cole scanned the many bodies sprawled out in the street. "Could be any one of 'em. The only witness we have, the manager, won't be able to confirm anything until the doc's checked him over."

"If he's one of the ones who got away, there'll be a reckoning." Roose chuckled. "They might even do our job for us."

"Somewhat wishful thinking there, Sterling. You'll need to hunt 'em down and bring 'em in, then we can get to the bottom of this damned fiasco."

"You're not coming?"

"Sterling, I've done my duty for the day," he sighed. "I'm supposed to be retired, remember?"

"You're too young to retire – besides, I need you."

"Nah, you don't need me, Sterling. You can call on Brown Owl, the Arapaho. He's the best tracker there is."

"Except he's not – you is."

"That's gracious of you, you old skunk," he grinned, "but I need to get back to Pa's place. He ain't too well. I'm not sure he's gonna be around much longer."

Deep in thought, Roose swung away for a moment. Already, bodies were being covered in white shrouds. Several burly men lifted them and stacked them in the back of a flat-bed wagon, destined for the undertakers.

"All right, Cole, if that's how it is."

"You're in safe hands with Brown Owl. He's a good friend, dependable and honest. I've known him for as long as I can remember so I have no worries about placing you in his good hands."

"Yeah, but I'll miss you, Cole."

"Now, don't get all maudlin on me, Sterling. How hard can it be to track down such an incompetent bunch as this?"

"Not very."

"Well, there you go. I'll see you back here in less than two days. Trust me."

"I hope you're right," said Roose and moved away, calling to several men lingering close by.

Cole watched his old friend swear in the men as deputies and couldn't prevent a shudder running through him, his sense of foreboding growing by the second. He couldn't understand why, but perhaps none of this was going to be as straightforward as he'd said it would.

CHAPTER THREE

The old place felt chill as he stepped inside, kicking off the dust from his boots. Hanging up his jacket on the hat stand in the hallway, he moved to the foot of the stairs and looked to the top. "Pa? Pa, are you awake? Got some news for you. From town." He started to climb then stopped as Marta, his father's loyal Mexican housekeeper, appeared from the rear kitchen, face screwed up in anguish.

"Oh, *Señor* Reuben," she said, words laced with tears, "it is *Señor* Martin, he is not eating and seems so weak. I wanted to call for the doctor, but I was too frightened to leave him." She broke down, and Cole went to her, holding her tight. Pressing her face against his chest, she sobbed uncontrollably.

Waiting for the right moment before he released her, Cole drew in a deep breath. "All right, Marta, I'll go to him now. You ride over to the Doc's and tell him to get here as soon as he can."

She scurried away, wringing her hands, muttering incoherent Spanish under her breath. Taking his time, dreading what he would find, Cole climbed the stairs.

His father's room was blanketed in darkness, the heavy

drapes shutting out all available light. A small oil lamp flickered pathetically in the far corner, and the air was heavy with the smell of sickness. The only sound was the awful, dry wheeze of his father's labored breathing.

Up until a year ago, his father's health had been robust. Often, he would be found out in the far reaches of his ranch, checking the fences, guiding any errant cattle back to the main herd, a herd which was due to be sold in only a few weeks' time. He'd return to the house, full of vim, grinning like an ape, happy to be alive.

After he'd moved in, Cole marveled at how sprightly his father was. "News was you ain't so good, Pa," he'd said on that first meeting. His father merely laughed for a reply.

Not anymore. Since then, his father's health had deteriorated until just, two weeks ago, he'd taken to his bed and had not yet moved, save for the occasional visit to the bathroom.

"I'm old, Reuben," he said only the other day. "I'm old and I *feel* old."

Here, standing at the foot of the large bed, squinting through the darkness, Cole studied his father and struggled to remember moments from the past. Good times, memories, shared events, but nothing would formulate in his mind. All he could picture was the mound of blankets and the irregular rise and fall of his father's chest.

This was not the man he knew. The man he knew was already gone. As if to confirm this idea, a low, pain-racked moan escaped from his father's lips. It subsided, and Cole stepped closer.

Spasmodically, his father would kick out under the covers, as if struggling against some invisible enemy, or a frantic attempt to free himself of the blankets. Cole knew not what it could be, only that his father was in pain, and there was nothing he could do.

When the call came from Sterling two days previously,

Cole had left without a word, not giving a second's thought for what he might find on his return. Yes, his father was old and tired, all tuckered out as the man himself might have said, but never did Cole think he would come home to this. Such a serious and sudden deterioration left him speechless and unable to know what to do. He'd always assumed, perhaps stupidly, that things would just go along the way they always had. That soon, his old Pa would recover, and life would return to its usual, dull routine. Normality.

The realization that those days had now come to an end made him numb.

Sitting down at the foot of the bed, he remained there until Marta returned with Doctor Henson. She might have been away for an hour or half a day, he couldn't tell. Like vague shadows, they fluttered around him, and he wandered outside as if in a dream and sat on the porch, rolled himself a cigarette, and waited.

It was Marta's strangled cries that brought him back to reality. He got up and went to go back inside. Doc Henson stood there, grim and serious. "I'm sorry, Reuben, I did all I could, but …"

He pressed a hand on Reuben's shoulder. Cole gave a tiny shrug and said, "Thanks anyway. I knew he was sick, but never how bad it truly was."

"Nobody did, except perhaps him. My guess, it was some sort of sickness in his brain. A cancer maybe, or something to do with his arteries."

"His what?"

"Blood vessels. That would account for his forgetfulness of late, his wandering around the house. Marta kept me informed when you were away. It's been a gradual but relentless decline, Reuben, but, like I say, no one knew. He was often lucid, and during those times, he was the same as he always was. At least, now he is at peace."

Cole stared, the guilt overwhelming him. He should have been here more often, spent more time with his father, savoring each precious moment. Now he never would. Life, as always, had turned another page.

"I'll see to all the arrangements, Reuben, so you have no need to worry. He'll be in the family plot, I'm guessing, up there with your mom?"

Cole grunted, shook the doctor's hand, and watched him ride off.

It was only when the sun went down that he returned indoors.

CHAPTER FOUR

S tanding on the boardwalk just outside the entrance to his dry goods store, Larry Grimes, face lifted skywards, took in the morning sunshine. With the furor of the failed bank robbery now in the past, the town had returned to normal. Several passers-by called out to him as they strolled along the street, and he would nod and smile, raising his hand occasionally. A popular man, almost everyone frequented his store at some point or other. Recently, the inclusion of a mail-order catalogue to his business attracted a growing number of fashion-conscious women, all keen to discover the latest 'best-thing' from out east. It was to this purpose that Florence Caitlin mounted the steps and bobbed her head in his direction.

"'Morning, Miss Caitlin."

"Good morning, Mr Grimes. Another beautiful day."

"Sure is, although I suspect that early morning chill I'm feeling is the precursor to winter coming on."

"That dreadful robbery was so very terrible, was it not? I hope you were not a witness to any of it?"

"No, miss, I give thanks I had not yet opened up when it

all erupted. So many killed, thankfully most of them those vile robbers. I have not yet heard much news, but I do know the Sheriff has gone to track them down."

"Let us hope it all ends well."

"Indeed," he said.

Smiling, she stepped inside, her patent leather boots clumping across the wood flooring. Larry watched her and sighed. If only he had the courage, he would invite Florence for a Sunday afternoon walk through the surrounding hills, or a buggy ride down to the river. Her cool, blue eyes, blonde ringlets and full, pouting mouth brought uncontrolled heat to his loins. However, he accepted he could never ask her to join him. Everyone in town, including Florence, knew his heart was set elsewhere, yet his roaming eye meant he might never be entirely satisfied with just one woman, no matter how attractive that one woman might be. Believing him to be steady, God-fearing man, nobody could tell what went on behind those soft, gentle brown eyes of his. Perhaps this knowledge was the reason why Florence appeared so comfortable in his presence. She believed him to be faithful, a good man, strong and virtuous. Handsome too, despite his limp. Perhaps if she knew the truth, she would no longer frequent his store. Nor, perhaps, would the majority of his customers. And Cathy, who held the flame close to his heart, may be forced to make up her mind and turn her back on him for good.

Pushing aside these disturbing thoughts, Larry shuffled inside. His leg felt good today, the warmth helping to ease the pain in his knee. The bullet he'd caught at Gettysburg had made him a virtual cripple for the last ten years and more, but his determination to walk unaided meant that few knew the history of his limp. Rumor had it he'd fallen from a horse some years back. Such a belief was fine by him, anything to divert them from the truth.

As he expected, Florence was at the catalogue stand, slowly leafing through the illustrations on the pages. She barely looked up as Larry moved up beside her. "I see they've added some new lines."

"Straight from Chicago, so they say."

"Chicago?" She looked at him. "Didn't you come from there, Mr Grimes?"

"I was born there, yes."

She arched a single eyebrow and stared at him intriguingly. "I've heard it say you joined the Army, Mr Grimes, fought for the Blues, that the horse you rode was shot under you and you suffered a broken knee."

"Something like that." He didn't add that the only factual part of her story was that he had fought for the Union, volunteering as soon as Lincoln made the call.

"You don't mind me asking you, do you?"

"No, not at all." He forced a small bark of a laugh. Had she noticed something in his changed mood, he wondered. He hastily did his best to sidetrack her. "It was all a long time ago, Miss Caitlin."

"Not all that long ago. Ten years. We're still healing."

"Yes, I guess that's so."

"The efforts made to try to reform the south into some form of social Utopia are failing miserably. Soon we'll be right back to where we started before the War even began."

"I can't see that happening, Miss Caitlin. I believe the President has it all under control."

"You think so? Then why didn't he send troops in to quell the outbreak of violence down in Mississippi that time? That Nathan Forrest had been stirring things for too long, in my opinion."

"I don't believe it was Forrest who instigated the violence in Mississippi."

"Possibly not, but it was all thanks to his creation of those lunatics called the Ku Klux Klan that this all started."

Larry Grimes blinked. "Your grasp of politics surprises me, Miss Caitlin."

"Why? Because I'm a woman?"

He side-stepped her caustic retort, continuing to smile despite the growing anxiety spreading through him. It was true; he himself saw similarities to how the country was back in the early 1860s. To think of it all exploding into armed confrontation once again would be enough to have him packing his bags and heading for Canada.

"No, not because you're a woman," he said, as disarmingly as he could. "Because of your passion."

"Passion? I'm not a secessionist, Mr Grimes. My father too fought in the War – for the Union."

"I didn't know that."

"He was killed at Second Manassas."

The unemotional matter-of-fact way she revealed this awful news shocked him. "I'm sorry," he said gently.

"Where did that bullet take down your horse, Mr Grimes?"

He wondered, not for the first time, whether or not he should tell her the truth. He drew in a breath. "Gettysburg."

Her eyes clouded over and then, quite unexpectedly, she reached over and squeezed his hand. "You're hiding something, Mr Grimes. I can tell."

Feeling the heat rise to his jawline, he cleared his throat and gave her a tiny nod. The conversation was growing too close for comfort. He gently tugged his hand free and moved over to the counter. "I'm glad you find that catalogue of interest, Miss Caitlin. Once you put your order in, they say six weeks is the waiting time. That's quite something."

"Indeed it is." She stared at him, waiting for him to continue, perhaps. When he didn't, she returned to the catalogue, wetting a slim index finger before recommencing her search through the many items on offer.

Some hours later, having replenished shelves and served at least a dozen or so customers, he stepped outside again. The street buzzed with people, many walking, some riding by on horses, the occasional buggy or wagon trundling along, wheels in need of grease grating around their axles. Larry blew out his breath and checked his fob-watch. Almost mid-afternoon. Cathy was usually here by now, and he wondered what might have prevented her from coming in. Her visits were the highlight of his day, although she probably didn't know how much he looked forward to her arrival. He never said anything. A woman like Cathy, strong, independent, wouldn't be interested in somebody like him – a virtual cripple. Perhaps he should try his luck with Florence. After all, she'd held his hand, which was something Cathy had never done in the whole two years he'd known her.

Checking both ends of the street, he returned to the store interior, his heart heavy, his mood low.

CHAPTER FIVE

"I'm gonna need to call a doctor," she said, placing the big cast-iron pot carefully upon the stovetop.

"You've done admirably so far," he said from inside the bedroom, propped up by every pillow she had.

"What's the matter," sensing something in his tone, "you don't want to get fixed?" She swung around and stared at him across the tiny cabin room.

"Of course I wanna get fixed."

"Well then."

"I just thought if I could lay up for a couple more days, I'd be fine."

"Fine you may be, but a doctor would know that for sure. That hole in your chest was deep, and the other one is all puckering up."

"You packed it with some stuff, didn't you? Weird stuff."

"I did, yes, but it smells, and I need to get it all cleaned out proper."

Collapsing his head back into the pillows, he blew out a long sigh. "Truth is, I'm scared. Scared they'll come back. If you were out fetching whoever and they burst in here ..."

"All right," she said gently, drying her hands on a rag and throwing it into the corner. Unrolling her sleeves, she moved across the room and entered the bedroom. She sat down on the bed beside him. "I think it's time you told me what went on and why they shot you."

"Do I have to?"

"Yes, you do. And I ain't gonna stop badgering you until you do."

"My, you are nothing but a terrier, ain't yeh."

"I am that. Funny, my husband used to call me that – *Cathy,* he'd say, *you has as much sand, spit, and venom as any rat-catchin' terrier there ever has been!*" She laughed hard and long, shaking her head, looking back through the years.

"I thought you said he was away," he said when, at last, she paused.

Her eyes, bright with the tears of laughter, hardened. "No. I said he was 'sort of'. He's away, but not in the strict meaning of the word. He's dead. Scarlet fever. Cut him down like he was a weak-kneed infant. I did all I could, Doc Henson, too. Up for three nights we was ..." Shaking her head again, but this time in a deep, heavy sadness, she pulled in a huge breath. "I lost him, and there ain't a day goes by that I wish he would come back."

"I'm sorry."

"Don't be – you never even knew him."

"Even so."

"Even so, it's your turn. Tell me your story, then I'll fetch the Doc again and we'll get you right."

He looked deep into her eyes for a moment before slowly turning away. A few deep breaths, as if he were preparing himself for some mighty physical effort, and then he launched himself into the story.

CHAPTER SIX

'We'd set to casing the bank for more than two weeks. A big deposit was coming in from the railroad, mostly gold transported to government storehouses. None of us knew how much, but Bernie Seagrams, our boss, if you wanna call him such, he'd caught a whiff of it from some drunkard over in Amarillo over a card game. He said it was somewhere in the region of fifty to a hundred thousand dollars. Life-changing. The thought of it made us determined to see it through.

'Bethlehem is a smallish town, past its best, but it is on the main railroad line from Chicago. We rode in two at a time, and Pete Mullins and me got ourselves a room in a two-bit hotel near the end of the main street. The plan was for us to wander around, keeping ourselves as inconspicuous as possible, whilst noting down the comings and goings at the bank.

'They'd brought in a group of new guards, well-armed, to protect the shipment. It was to be stored overnight before continuing on its long journey to somewhere deep in Texas. We had no idea where it was headed, and neither did we care.

'We was on the boardwalk of the saloon, chomping on cheroots, when we first saw him. At the time, I had no idea who he was. Tall and lean, grey pin-striped trousers and black tailcoat. He wore his gun across his belly. The star on his lapel was huge, as if he were proclaiming himself as to just who exactly he was – the law.

'Pete grumbled under his breath, saying he would be the first to die as he looked as mean as a coyote. I agreed. I do not think I have ever seen such a look on a man's face as the one he bore. Until his partner arrived. That was when I got scared.

'Something started niggling away at me that this was going to be a darn sight more difficult than Seagrams had ever thought.

'I learned later that the lean one in black was Sterling Roose, sheriff of the town. His companion, dressed in buckskins, was an Army Scout name of Reuben Cole. They had something of a reputation these two, both of 'em as hard as the land upon which they rode. Men who knew about killin' and made light of it with a detached indifference that was chilling.

'The day of the delivery came, and Seagrams met with me outside a millinery shop. I told him of my concerns, and he laughed them off. He was a man on a mission, and nothing was about to force him away from what he saw as his destiny.

'"I'm gonna be rich, as rich as I have ever dreamed of!" He said this with his thumbs stuck in his belt, looking as happy as a little boy on his birthday.

'That was that. Disregarding all I said, the time came for us to go in. Six of us, bandanas over our noses, we went steaming inside, six-guns ready. Three others were outside, two with the horses, old Joey Steiner driving the wagon. The tellers behind the counter were already thrusting their hands upwards as Seagrams shouted, "Get your money from those drawers and don't even think about trying anything foolish!"

'Vaulting the counter, Jonas and I burst into the tiny office at the back where we found a suited man sporting a resplendent handlebar moustache and a quivering look. "We want the combination to the safe," spat Jonas and rammed his sixgun hard into the man's forehead.

'The bank at Bethlehem was one of the new-fangled types imported from Germany. Not only was it large, but it boasted a twin set of combination locks, both of which had to be properly engaged for the great, heavy door to open.

'From the look on his face, I could see the bank manager was not the bravest of men. He gladly gave up the combination, and I set to it while Jonas kept the gun to his head.

'I hollered as the tumblers engaged, and Seagrams came in, beaming. Together with myself and two others, we set to filling the many canvas sacks we'd brought with us. Gradually, an impressive mound of money bags grew beside the safe, and soon we'd be taking them to the wagon outside.

'It was then, perhaps when he saw us begin to take the money away, that the little bank manager said something. "You won't get away with this. That is railroad money, destined for the government. They will hunt you down and hang you all."

'Jonas hit him, the sound of his pistol against the side of his skull making the most fearful crack. The force of the blow tipped him out of his revolving chair and sent him into the far corner, blood already streaming, his moans growing louder by the second. "I'll put a bullet in you if you don't stop," shouted Jonas as Seagrams, distracted from the money for a moment, drew his own gun, and aimed it. "Shut up!"

'The poor man, stricken by pain and fear, did the exact opposite, his moaning becoming a loud wail. A horrible sound, it travelled way beyond the walls of the bank and was better than any alarm to warn the town of what was happening.

'It was then I did a most foolhardy thing. I stepped between the manager and those two fools with their guns. Waving my hands, I shouted, "There is no need for any killin'!"

'If not already incensed, those two became like wild dogs, frothing at the mouth, teeth chomping, eyes flashing. "Get out the damned way," screamed Jonas, but I wouldn't. Behind me, the little manager's yells were continuing, and they were awesome loud. I could see what was stirring behind Jonas' eyes and what I saw scared me, I don't mind telling you. I knew him to be a low life, a simpleton who was quick to violence, so I took no chances. In that tiny lull, with uncertainty dancing across his features, I pulled my gun and shot him high up on his gun arm.

'Everything went crazy from that point.

'As Jonas cartwheeled across the room, Seagrams' jaw hung wide open. All of his plans, all of his dreams, were disintegrating right before his eyes, and I knew he was about to do something awful.

'So I shot him too, not in the arm this time, in the chest. I blew him flat against the far wall and watched him slide down to the ground, his eyes already lifeless, the hole in his body trailing smoke and blood.

'The bank manager's jaw hung open with disbelief at what he had witnessed. Although in obvious pain, his face swelling like a ripe melon, he no longer moaned. Ignoring him, and without another thought, I grabbed up three or four of them money sacks and rushed out into the main room.

'"What is going on in there," one of the gang demanded.

'"Bank manager shot Seagrams," I said quickly. "We have to go."

'No one took to questioning me as the four of us

remaining rushed out to join the rest of the gang outside. Grabbing handfuls of money, we stuffed dollar bills into the sacks while we ran. We threw some of the sacks into the back of the wagon. One or two of us went to tie bundles behind our saddles before we jumped onto the backs of our horses and made to high tail it out of there.

'Until Roose appeared.

'He stood in the centre of the street, Henry in his hand, aiming it like it was a turkey shoot, he was so damned calm. His first bullet took out old Joey Steiner, blowing him clean out of his seat. The horses went wild, rearing up, whinnying and squealing in terror, and stampeded down the street. There was nothing we could do but watch. Second bullet took the skull off one of the others, showering those closest to him with his blood and brains. That set off everyone, the hollering of both men and horses sounding like something from the very bowels of hell where tormented souls ranted and raved in the depths of their tortured souls.

'For that was what it was like. Pure hell.

'I was battling to keep my horse under control. Others were moving past me, swearing and cursing, beating at their horses with hands, hats, even drawn weapons. Anything to get those terrified beasts moving.

'More bullets raced through the air, missing some of us by mere inches. The air filled with horse sweat and fear. One or two of us sent some returning shots, but they was as ineffective as they was desperate. Struggling to move forward, I managed to pull my weapon and did my best to aim, but it was useless, my horse too far gone in fear by now.

'The other one came out of a side street. Reuben Cole. I don't know how he did that, sneaking up on us without being seen, but he shot another of our gang dead and wounded Jim-Bob Winters in the leg before we managed to gallop away from that killing zone.

'We were in a sorry state. Four of us dead, Jonas wounded back in the bank, poor little Jim-Bob squealing like a stuck pig beside me. I knew he wouldn't last the night, but there was nothing I or anyone else could do. Our only thought now was to ride, hard and fast, back to our hideout, count whatever money we had, and make our way down to the Mexican border and safety.

'When finally we made it to our camp, the horses blown, all of us in a wretched state of mangled nerves, I did what I could to make Jim-Bob comfortable. With the afternoon drawing on and the heat gripping us like a vice, I took a hot knife to little Jim-Bob's thigh and dug that slug out. We packed it with tequila-soaked rags, and I sat with him as he writhed around in his blanket, consumed by sweat. The others drank what little liquor remained, smoked and mumbled. All of us were numb with shock. We had little to show for all of our efforts, and I was the only one still alive who'd managed to put some money in my saddlebags.

'It was in the early evening when Jonas appeared. As the others whooped and hollered with relief and excitement, I stood like a rock. Our eyes bore into one another. His right arm dangled useless by his side but in his left hand was his Colt.

'I took my chance and bolted, leaping onto the back of my horse as the first bullet pinged over my head. Keeping low, I set off, knowing full well they would be behind me.

'They caught up with me by a trickling brook, and there they shot me, stripped me and left me for dead. It was justice, said Jonas, his eyes alight with murderous glee. "I'll see you in Hell, you traitorous wretch," he said and spat at me before riding off.

'I passed out, and when I woke up, I was in a cabin with the most beautiful woman I've ever seen tending to me. And that's it. The whole thing. I do not know what will become of me now, but it cannot be as bad as what I have already been through during that miserable attempt to rob the bank.'

He lowered his head and blew out a long sigh, seemingly exhausted with the re-telling.

Having listened in silence, Cathy leaned back in her chair and considered the man sitting across from her at the rough-hewn table. He chose to focus on the floor.

"Is that the truth?" she said after some time.

"I swear it is."

"Not sure if a self-confessed bank robber's word is all that believable."

"I understand that, but why would I lie? You saved my life. I owe you."

That was good enough for Cathy. She got up, made coffee and eggs, serving them up on tin plates, and he ate like he hadn't tasted food in days. This brought a smile to her lips, and she felt he was a good man, one to be trusted. Unlike her late husband, whose wanderlust brought her nothing but heartache, despite her loving the very bones of him.

CHAPTER SEVEN

They reined in on the rise overlooking the tired, worn-out collection of warped wooden buildings that someone had once christened the town of 'Haven'. One of the men spat and swore. "This looks deader than a graveyard, Jonas."

"Graveyards ain't dead, only those in 'em."

"You know what I mean."

"All I need is a doctor to patch me up, then we'll be gone." To give some emphasis to his words, he attempted to revolve his shoulder, an action which brought a string of obscenities to his lips. "It's been two days, and I feel it going numb."

"That's good, ain't it? No more pain."

"Are you stupid or you just ain't got a brain."

"Ah shucks, Jonas, no need to say such things to me!"

"*Gringo,*" said the Mexican who sat astride his horse on the other side of Jonas, "if you don't like it, stay here and cook us some food."

"Food? Hell, I ain't your servant, Cruces! Besides, we ain't got no food."

"That's another reason to go take a look," said the fourth

member of the gang, a gangly, pock-marked youth with no teeth.

Jonas kicked his horse and eased it down the incline, the others slowly moving in behind.

The sun burned, but not as ferociously as of late. The year was turning, the nights much colder now than they had been. Soon, snow would come and travelling across country would become increasingly difficult. They needed supplies and a place to stay, lick their wounds, and reassess their situation. These thoughts, among others, buzzed around inside Jonas' head. None of this was his fault. The plan had been down to Seagrams, but however clever their former leader was, he made no back-up plan, never considering for a moment anything would go wrong. Now the gang had to somehow extricate itself and move on, and this time, whatever plan evolved, it would succeed. It would be Jonas' plan, if he ever got this arm fixed. He tried clenching and unclenching his fist but could barely manage it, the numbness spreading with frightening rapidity. He pushed aside dark, unsettling thoughts and spurred his horse into a canter.

The single saloon was a sad affair, a single narrow room with four tables and a battered staircase leading to rooms above. Around one table, two men studied torn, dog-eared playing cards. Behind the counter, a tiny, bald man polished glasses. He looked up as the four dust-spattered riders came inside. All at once, his hands started to tremble.

"Easy," said Jonas through clenched teeth, "we is tired, thirsty, and hungry. All we want is to rest up for a spell."

"You got beer?" asked the gangly youth.

The man nodded. "It's cold too."

The youth slapped the countertop with his palm. "Then serve 'em up!"

The bald barkeep disappeared into a backroom. Jonas gave the room a scan and stepped up to the two card players. He doffed his hat. "Gentlemen, would there be a doctor hereabouts?"

The men studied Jonas' blood-soaked arm and shifted uneasily in their chairs. "Doc Farlow is retired now," said one of them, "but he still lives above Maisie's."

"Maisie's?"

"That's our local whorehouse," said the bald man, reappearing with a tray of four beer glasses filled to the top, froth cascading down the sides.

"It ain't in operation any longer," put in the card-player quickly.

While the others attacked their beer, Jonas' eyes never left the two men. "How far?"

"Straight down the street. You can't miss it, the sign's still hanging there. You get to Doc Farlow's by the steps outside. That's where he lodges."

"Obliged," said Jonas, crossed to his beer and downed it in one gulp. Smacking his lips and belching loudly, he went to the door. "I won't be long, boys."

"You want someone to come with you?"

Jonas smiled at the gangly youth. "I'll be all right, Len, but thanks for offering."

Stopping at the foot of the wooden staircase, attached as it was to the abandoned whorehouse, Jonas hesitated. The steps were grey, and the warped planks did not look as if they could take the weight of a child, let alone a man. A rotten door at the top hung on rusted hinges. No sign of life.

Jonas tentatively placed his foot on the first step and winced as it groaned. Applying more of his weight, he began a slow, laborious ascent, pausing, testing the planks one at a time before moving up to the next.

With one more step to go, he levered up his foot. The old door wrenched open, and a small, rotund man wearing stained long johns appeared holding a Navy Colt in his hand.

Surprised by this sudden apparition appearing before him, Jonas jumped back, screamed, lost his footing and tipped over backwards down the steps, splintering several, until he hit the bottom and rolled across the ground, throwing up billowing clouds of grey dust, which slowly settled over him. He lay motionless, aware of the pain spreading through his body, not only from the gunshot wound, but new, even more excruciating rivals from bruises, cuts, and, more than likely, breaks.

"What, in the name of Hades, is you doing creeping up my stairs, boy?"

Aware of the voice, but not its direction, Jonas dared not move. He felt if he did, he would snap his spine in two. Breathing into the dirt, trying not to take too much into his mouth, he groaned, "Help me."

"How can I help you, you darned fool? You've gone and busted my staircase. Now I can't get down nor up."

"Ah no, Lemmy," came the voice of a young woman, "now we're gonna just have to stay in bed all day." She giggled.

"And what about food and water, eh? This darned fool has condemned us to a jail sentence."

"It ain't that bad, is it, Lemmy? Being locked up with me?"

"Ah, Maisie, you know I would wanna spend the rest of my days locked up with you."

Another giggle, the sound of something striking the girl's body, and then the crash of the old door closing behind them, muffled cries coming from within.

Jonas groaned. The old coot had left him out here to die. If he ever got back on his feet, he'd get him to patch up the wounds then put a forty-five caliber bullet through his brainpan.

———

Sometime later, concerned over Jonas' whereabouts, the others moved outside, ambling down the street to find their leader sprawled in the dust, barely breathing. Len broke into a run and got down beside him. "Jonas," he said, shaking his fallen boss by the shoulders. "Jonas, is you dead?"

"Somebody shot him?" asked the Mexican Cruces, drawing his gun and scanning all sides of the street. Len quickly checked Jonas' body and shook his head. "Channi," said Cruces, looking back the way they had come, "cover the far end, and I'll try and see who is in that doctor's place."

"Who did this?" demanded Channi. He peered down the deserted street. "I'll kill 'em when I see 'em."

Reaching the broken steps, Cruces gave a low cackle and eased his flat-crowned sombrero from his forehead with the barrel of his revolver. "No one, *mi amigo*. He fell down these stairs." He pushed a step with his boot and went clean through. He laughed again. "They are rotten. All of them. I wonder who it is who lives there?"

"A doctor, so that chump back in the saloon said." Len cradled Jonas' head, smoothing away strands of hair from his boss's sweating brow. "I don't like the look of him, Cruces," he said, his voice whining. "Call out to that doc and tell him to get down here."

"I do not think anyone will be coming down here anytime soon, *amigo*."

They all heard it then, an outburst of gleeful laughter, the slap of naked flesh, followed by prolonged moans.

"What the..." Cruces brought up his gun and took a bead on the door latch. Holding his breath, he eased off one carefully aimed shot and blew the latch clean off, the retort of the blast echoing throughout the quiet, empty streets.

A terrific hollering and squawking emitted from beyond the door, and soon it was ripped open, a small, disheveled, sweat-drenched man appearing, face twisted into a scowl of pure, uncontained anger.

Before he could speak, however, Cruces' next shot tore into the top of the door frame, inches away from the old man's bald head. Yelling out in alarm, the old man dipped back inside, hands waving above his head. "I'm unarmed, I'm unarmed!"

"Get back out here, you old coot." Cruces loosed off another shot, tearing out a huge chunk of the nearside door-frame. "The next bullet is going right through your wall!"

"Cruces," called Channi from behind him.

"What?" demanded Cruces, without turning, keeping his gun trained on the door.

"Cruces, come here *now*!"

Swinging around red-faced, Cruces spat out several choice words, ending with, "What is it?"

He saw Channi doing a strange little dance as he pointed down the street. Cruces followed his companion's outstretched finger and swallowed down a gasp.

"We got trouble," said Len, standing up.

"Looks that way," said Cruces, replacing the two spent cartridges with fresh ones. Holstering his gun, he took in a breath. "I sure hope this don't take long. Jonas needs tending to."

CHAPTER EIGHT

C athy came back inside having hitched up her horse to the buggy. Tugging on a thick overcoat, she arched an eyebrow towards her guest and sighed, not liking the way he struggled getting dressed one bit. "Are you fit for travelling? The air is becoming sharp."

"I'll be fine," he said. He'd managed to pull on trousers and shirt from her husband's wardrobe she had so methodically laundered and repaired as he slept. He winced as he pushed his arm through a sleeve. "I can feel it. The infection. Smell it too."

"Well, the doc will sort it, I am sure. I am thinking we cut across to Haven, which is closer. Doc Farlow is a smelly old goat, but he is a good doctor, so everyone says. After my man died, they all told me he is better than the doc over in Bethlehem." She bit down hard on her bottom lip. "Wish I'd known that at the time."

"Perhaps nobody could have done much for him."

"In the end, I think you're right."

He hobbled towards her. She took him by the elbow and led him outside. Immediately, he took to shivering. The sky, no longer blue, was a uniform white, the promise of snow in the air. She'd put one of her husband's overcoats on the buckboard, and, after helping him to step up, she got in beside him and put the coat around his shoulders.

"I'm obliged you doing this for me, Miss Catherine."

"Just Catherine is fine." She shot him a smile. "You never did tell me yours."

"Ah, yeah ... it's Norton," he said, not too convincingly.

"Norton?" He nodded. "Well, if that's your real name or not, pleased to make your acquaintance." She thrust out a gloved hand, and he took it, laughing, an action which soon sent him into a bout of hoarse, raspy coughing. "We need to get moving. You'll be overcome with fever soon." She flicked the reins and they trundled away over the hard, rutted ground, picking up the trail to Haven within barely ten minutes.

Some way out of the town, the horse straining in the harness with its unusual load of two people, they first heard the gunshots. Cathy reined in the horse, which blew out its nostrils loudly with relief. They sat, listening.

"You have a gun?"

She looked at him. "Only the old Henry, here behind me."

"We might need it."

Distant shots rang out, sounding like tacks being dropped into a bucket. "Wonder what it is."

"I don't know, Cathy, but I don't think I am up for any gunplay." He gave a wry smile. "Unless pushed."

Again, she looked, harder this time. Drawn, sweating profusely, his pallor sickly grey, she could see he was deteriorating fast. She also knew she had to get him to the doctor's before he succumbed to the developing fever, the poison running freely through him, bringing him ever closer to death. "Listen, I want you to wrap yourself up in that coat. Put your head down and try and stay conscious."

"Thought you said sleep was a good thing?"

"Mostly it is, but right now, you need to stay awake and focus on fighting that fever. You look like death."

"I *feel* like death."

"All righty," she said, twisting in her seat to pick up the Henry. She worked the lever and engaged a fresh round.

"You sure you know how to use that thing?"

"I do indeed."

"You said that with meaning."

Nodding, her eyes misted over as she looked back to that dreadful day not so very long ago when they came. Three of them, stick thin, starving to death by the look of them, their black eyes smoldering from faces ravaged with hunger. Nevertheless, despite this, they moved with mesmerizing grace, sweeping around the log-cabin from different angles. Two had Winchesters, the third a bow, arrow nocked. Jude, who had been out turning potatoes in one of the small vegetable patches when he noticed them, was already running faster than a roadrunner, hollering, "Get the Henry, Cathy!"

Old Beth, their dog, such a faithful, sweet-natured thing, was snarling, showing her teeth. She made a charge for the nearest Indian, launching herself with mindless courage at his throat. He tried to bat her away with the Winchester, holding it by the barrel, but she was determined, that old dog. She got her teeth around his forearm, and they fell to the hard earth in a mess of screams and growls.

The blood spurted from his mangled arm, the Winchester forgotten. Old Beth held on, those teeth sinking ever deeper, shaking him as if he were one of the rats she often killed in the barn.

The one with the bow did for Old Beth, shooting her in the flank with two arrows. Cathy always thought, perhaps truly, that this was the reason why she took out the old Henry from the buggy with such determination, ignored Jude's anguished pleas for her to give it to him, and shot that Indian with the bow right through the head. Without a pause, she put three more bullets into another coming around the well, doing his best to shoot her with his Winchester. He went down and stayed down.

"Cath!"

She shouldered him out the way, working the lever, and strode towards the maimed warrior on the ground. Naked, body alive with sweat and blood, he writhed around in agony, blabbering something to her, a look of abject terror on his face. She silenced him with the remainder of the rifle's load, perforating his torso and enjoying every shot.

"Yes," she said slowly, dragging herself back to the present. "I surely do mean it." And she twitched the reins and urged her poor, bedraggled horse towards town.

CHAPTER NINE

F our riders, black dust coats enveloping their bodies, black hats crammed down upon their heads, masking features, designed to instill fear. They rode with a deliberate, slow advance as if they were well-rehearsed in this sort of intimidation.

Channi edged up close to Cruces. The Mexican stood with his six-gun drawn, eying the approaching riders with increasing anxiety. "They look mean. Twin guns, tied down, they are gunfighters."

"We can handle 'em, Cruces, don't worry."

"But I do," said Cruces. "Wish we had rifles."

"I have my Winchester back with the horses," said Len. "I could pick 'em off with ease if that is what you think we should do."

Looking down at Jonas' inert body, Channi drew in a deep breath. "Jonas would know what to do."

"I say we spread out," said Len. "Cruces, you stay here. Channi, over there to the right, behind those stacked barrels next to the old assayer's office. Me, I'll run back to my horse and put a line on 'em with my Winchester."

"Shoot, Len, you got it all worked out," said Channi, voice buoyant, suitably impressed.

"Do as he says," snarled Cruces from the corner of his mouth. "Meanwhile, I'll talk to 'em, see what it is they want."

"They is Ed Rollins' men," came a voice, and the all looked up to see the doc, on all fours, poking his head out of his door. "I don't know who you boys is, but my advice is to go back to where you came from. Rollins is not a man who takes kindly to strangers, especially those ones who try to shoot up his town."

"*His* town?" Channi chuckled. "If this is his town, he is welcome to it."

"Wasn't always like this. Once it was a thriving, lively place, plenty of money being spent by gold-miners. When the seam was spent, they left. Rollins stayed behind, invested his money wisely, and is now trying to come to some arrangement with the railroad companies. If he succeeds, this town will boom once again."

"I hear that story almost every place I go," said Channi. "There must be more busted up towns than there is flies around a dead body."

"There'll be flies around Jonas if we don't act fast," put in Len. He swung around and dashed back towards his horse.

The riders continued to move inexorably forward, but this sudden burst of activity from Len spurred them into action. Raising their hats, they beat their horses' flanks and broke into a sudden charge.

"Ah hell," growled Cruces and brought up his revolver, fanning the hammer, spurting out a blaze of lead with no effect whatsoever.

Diving behind the stacked barrels, as he was told to do, Channi took his time, gathering his thoughts, controlling his body as the palpitations grew into something closer to hammer blows in his chest. Holding his breath, he rested his gun arm on the top of the closest barrel and eased off shots, one after the other, watching with some satisfaction as one of the riders rose up, clutching at his chest, pitching backwards over his saddle, blood bursting from the wound. He hit the dirt hard and lay still. Channi hollered in his triumph and fed in more cartridges as the riders fanned out in a wide arc.

Meanwhile, Len had reached his horse and scrambled around in pulling out the Winchester from its scabbard. Working the lever, he rested the barrel across the back of his horse and carefully aimed. When he squeezed the trigger, another rider dropped, and Len, not the most vociferous of people, grunted in satisfaction as he prepared to fire again.

Cruces did not fare so well. After leaping over Jonas' inert form, he sprinted towards the ruined steps. He did his best to keep himself low, but the riders were close now. Although their mounts were increasingly out of control due to the gunshots, one of them managed to put a bullet into Cruces' thigh. The Mexican squealed and tumbled sideways, his Colt skidding across the ground, well out of his reach. Clutching at the wound, he tried to shuffle backwards, but before he managed to retreat less than six feet, the two remaining riders were upon him.

Channi, his gun now reloaded despite spilling some of the bullets onto the ground, groaned in anguish at the sight of poor Cruces. Why wasn't Len shooting more rounds? He glanced back down the street and swore when he saw the answer to his question.

Three more riders were approaching from the other side of town. Len was doing his best to react after he'd got wind of their advance, turning, dropping to one knee, lining up the first target. Unfortunately for Len, they were so quiet that now they were virtually upon him. They surrounded him, guns drawn, letting him know with little doubt he was a dead man as soon as he fired his Winchester. He didn't debate the situation for long, and, throwing the Winchester down, he stood up, arms raised.

"You've shot down two of my boys," said the closest rider to the squirming Cruces. "If they is dead, we will hang you. If they is sorely wounded, we'll strip you, whip you, and send you back from whatever hole you crawled out of. Tab, check their bodies."

Tab slowly dismounted. Taking his chance, Channi stepped out from behind the barrels.

"You put that gun away, boy," said the one doing all the talking, "unless you wanna meet your maker within the next ten seconds."

It didn't take those ten seconds for Channi to make up his mind and let his gun drop from trembling fingers.

"My name is Edward Rollins, and this is my town," said the talker and eased himself from the saddle. "Tab, how are them boys of mine?"

Tab, checking the rider that Channi had shot for any vital signs, let out a long sigh. "He's shot up bad, Mr Rollins."

"Yes, but is he dead?"

"Not yet, sir."

"All right, now check Louden there."

Louden was the poor rider who received the Winchester round from Len. There was a fair-sized hole in his chest, and his eyes were wide open. Tab didn't need to check further. "Nope, Mr Rollins, he's dead."

Upon hearing this, Rollins let out a prolonged sigh, pushed back his hat, and allowed himself a few seconds before he said, "That is a shame. He was a good man. Knew his mother. Knew her well. Thank the Lord she is also dead; otherwise, my wrath would be such that already I would be putting you bunch of vermin in the ground!"

The additional riders had by now steered Len to join the others. A frightened, pathetic figure, he wrung his hands constantly, features strained, already surrendering to the terrible inevitability of his impending doom.

"All right, boys," said Rollins, looking around him as if he were searching for something. "String 'em up."

CHAPTER TEN

From his saddle, Sterling Roose watched as Brown Owl, on hands and knees, studied the land. For all his years of riding with the Army, tracking down renegades and Comanche war-parties, Roose had never developed such a high level of skill as Cole and Brown Owl demonstrated. They were masters of their art, Cole especially. He could tell an escapee's direction from a single broken blade of grass. Now, watching Brown Owl, he was filled with the same sense of wonder as the scout stood, dusting off his buckskin trousers. "They ride fast, but here," he waved his hand over a broken up piece of hard, dry ground, "another is behind them. Not so fast. Perhaps his horse is old, or he is sick, maybe wounded."

"That would tie in with what happened back at the bank. The one who escaped through the back, he was wounded. Bad, so the bank manager said."

Brown Owl grunted and nodded, but did not answer. He swung himself up onto his pony's back. "They are not so far."

"Well then," Roose turned to his motley posse, "make sure your guns are loaded, men. It won't be long now."

Something rippled through them. A nervousness which you could almost taste. Roose looked away and wished, not for the first time, that Cole was riding with him.

A little farther on, they came to the remains of a camp. It didn't take long before Brown Owl pointed out the areas where the ground was scuffed and broken. "I think one rode away, with others close behind."

"An argument of kinds," said Roose, hands on the pommel, staring out across the endless plain. "That could work to our advantage."

"Don't see how," said one of the posse.

"It might mean we have less of 'em to tangle with."

"Tangle?" The man looked to his companions then back to Roose, panic in his voice. "You never said nothin' about tangling with anyone."

"Don't worry yourself none, Coltrane, I doubt it'll be so bad that we'll be calling on your superior firearm skills."

"Then what will you be calling on, Sheriff?" asked another.

"Who can tell? You're something of a lawyer, ain't you, Philips?"

"I was in law school before my daddy said they needed me back home to help pay the bills."

"But you know a little about the law?"

"A little. I studied in Chicago. A mighty fine city, I can tell you. It was my dream to open up my own little law—"

"I might just call on you to explain to our motley bank robbers the enormity of their crimes. How's about that?"

Philips didn't look impressed. Ignoring him, Roose turned again to Brown Owl. "Which way?"

In silence, Brown Owl mounted his pony and set off.

. . .

Slowing down, Brown Owl in the lead, they inched their way across the sad trickle that used to be a river and reined in when the Indian scout slipped down from his mount into the mud and raised his hand.

Roose leaned forward. "What you found?"

For a few anxious moments, Brown Owl continued to read the signs, so deep in concentration it seemed he had not heard Roose's question.

"Maybe he can't see anything," said one of the others, holding back with his two companions.

"Shut up, Knott," spat Roose, "when you got something sensible to say, then you can say it."

"You can't talk to me that way, Sheriff! I volunteered for this and I can walk away any time I choose."

"You do that and I'll hunt you down and throw you into jail!"

The air grew chilly. Knott fumed, face screwed up in a mix of confusion and indignation. His companions averted their eyes and stayed quiet.

"You is what is known as a dictator," said Knott, voice cracking.

"And you is what is known as an idiot, now quiet down before I knock you down."

"There's more," said the scout, continuing to examine the surroundings. "Someone else was here, on foot. Then, more tracks leading in two directions." He stood up and pointed. "Riders went that way. More than two of them. The one on foot took another direction."

"All right," said Roose. "We'll visit the one who was on foot first. They may be able to tell us what went on here. Boys, keep your wits about you."

As things turned out, there was no need for any caution because the small cabin they came upon not very long afterwards, with its small vegetable patch, little barn, and fenced in paddock, was empty. Blowing out his cheeks, Roose turned from pounding on the door to look at his men. "Seems like we follow the riders, boys."

This news did not inspire anyone, but they moved away nevertheless, falling in behind Brown Owl, who constantly checked the ground, until they came to the rise that overlooked a ramshackle town which appeared to be dead.

Until they heard the gunshots.

CHAPTER ELEVEN

"Kicking my heels around this place ain't gonna change my mood," said Cole, going through the papers in his father's desk. "I can't make head nor tail of any of this."

"I will do it, *Señor* Reuben," said Marta, her voice thick with grief.

"Most of it relates to cattle and horse deals from half a lifetime ago." He sat back and looked at the mound of paperwork in despair. "Marta, I reckon most of this could be burned."

"He was a great hoarder, your father," she said, lifted a little by the memory. "I think he felt that he may need these things again another day, so he kept them, just in case."

Running a hand through his hair, Cole gave a long sigh. "I should have gone with Sterling. I'm not ready for this sort of thing."

"You must go if you feel it is your duty," she said and gestured to the papers. "I can deal with this."

"I think I just might do that, Marta, if you're sure it's all right with you?"

A tiny flush spread across her cheeks. "*Señor* Reuben, this is your home now. You make the decisions."

"Well … Look, I been thinking. You've lived and worked here almost all your life." He noted her eyes widening, and the way she suddenly held her breath. She appeared to be preparing herself for some bad news. "Marta, if you can, I'd like you to continue working here. I'm not much of a one for—"

Marta gave out a great whoop and threw herself at him, covering his face with kisses. "Oh, *Señor* Reuben, I thought you were going to dismiss me – throw me out!"

"Please, Marta." He managed, with some effort, to extricate himself from her embrace. "Of course I'm not going to do that! No, I need you, Marta. Now more than ever."

As if realizing what she had done, she leaned back, hand covering her mouth, tears tumbling down her cheeks. "*Señor* Reuben, forgive me, I never meant—"

Suppressing his laughter, Cole stood up. "Hey, Marta, don't worry. I'm kinda touched at your reaction." Feeling the heat on his face, he touched his cheeks where she'd kissed him. "I'm never gonna say 'no' to your kisses!"

She gaped at him, and he swung away and strode out of the house before he said anything more.

At the jail, old Clancy Hughes was picking at his few remaining teeth when Cole came in. Dressed in buckskins and high boots, with his Colt Cavalry angled across his middle for a cross-belly draw, he was ready to ride out across the plains once more.

On seeing him, Clancy sat bolt upright, desperate to clear away the remnants of his chicken dinner. "Why, Mr Cole, sir. I was not expecting you."

"Me neither."

Frowning, Clancy took particular care with the almost empty bottle of whisky beside his dinner plate. "Eh? I don't get you."

"Never mind. Where's the prisoner?"

"In the back. Doc Henson patched him up real good. One of the other wounded fellas died. Didn't say a word."

Grunting, Cole went through the heavy door that opened up into a narrow passage. There were four cells, three of which were empty. At the far end, on the left, he found the one surviving bank robber curled up on a sagging wooden bunk, a threadbare blanket covering him. Cole pressed his face up close to the cell bars and coughed. The man did not stir. Cole raised his breath, his voice filling the small jail as he shouted, "Hey, pigswill, wake up!"

Startled, the man rolled over, the blanket forgotten, and sat up, rubbing his eyes. "Who in the name of—"

"Name is Cole, and I'm here to ask you some questions, which you would be advised to answer truthfully. Understand?"

"Questions?" The man, who could not have been more than eighteen years of age, swung his legs over the side of the bunk and put his face in his hands. "Mister, I can barely remember my own name."

"But you do remember shooting up that bank, don't you?"

His face came up, and he peered at Cole, the beginning of real, noticeable fear twitching at his face. "I doubt there'd be much point in denying that."

"Seeing as we've got about a hundred witnesses, I'd say that was sensible."

"But I have little recollection of what happened. Very little, in fact. I remember being shot and hitting the ground, but after that ..." He shook his head. "Sorry."

"What I need you to focus on is the fact that people died. That makes you an accessory."

"A what?"

"An *accessory*. It means you is just as much to blame for what went down as the men who pulled the triggers."

"I didn't shoot nobody, Mister, I swear to God."

"Like I said, in *law*, you is as much to blame as anyone else."

"But no, that can't be!" He jumped up and rushed to the bars, so fast and unexpected, Cole was forced to take a step back, hand instinctively dropping to his gun. "You can't do this. I never killed nobody in my life. Seagrams said to me we would be straight in and straight out, nothing about no killings."

"Seagrams? So this Seagrams was your leader, eh?"

Ashen-faced, the young man retreated a few steps, hands up in surrender. Clearly he'd realized some terrible mistake. "I never said no such thing. I didn't know him so well."

"Son, you have no need to worry. Seagrams, if he was the one led the robbery, is dead."

The young man's relief was clear. "Oh my."

"But there was someone else with him, in the bank manager's office. Who might that be?"

"I don't know, mister. I was outside."

"Outside or in, you must have some idea."

"No, sir, I don't."

"Tell you what, son, you give me your best bet on who it was, and I'll talk to the judge, tell him how well you cooperated in our investigations."

A slight hesitation followed. The young man chewed away at his lip, slumped down on the bunk, and stared. It took him quite a while before his head came around again. "You mean it? You will take away this – what was it? Accessory?"

"I can make it go away, son. Easy as easy is."

"You swear it?"

"As God's my maker."

This had the desired effect. The young man nodded his head several times and said, in a quiet voice, "Jonas. He was Seagrams' chosen one, if you put it that way."

"Jonas who?"

The young man's face came up. "That I don't know, Mister. I only ever knew him as Jonas."

"Well, that don't tell me much. I doubt I will be able to find out anything about him by just that. But never mind," he made an exaggerated yawn, "I'm sure the judge will do what he can...but no promises." He smiled, winked, and turned away.

"Wait!" cried the young man, rushing to the bars again, clinging onto them, face close, panic written into every line. "Falkin. His name is Jonas Falkin." He swallowed hard. "If you mean what you say, I have something else too."

Arching a single eyebrow, Cole moved closer and listened to what the young man had to say. Satisfied, Cole's smile grew wide. He tipped his hat's brim and returned to the outer room.

Clancy stood up as the scout returned. "You got what you needed?"

"I sure did. Don't suppose you happen to know who will be the judge for the trial of that boy?"

"I reckon it'll be Justice Hartley. He's tough. He's also a personal friend of the bank manager."

"Well, well, the world is full of surprises."

"I don't fully understand what you mean, Mr Cole."

"That's all right, Clance. Just means it'll be a quick trial is all."

"He has a reputation as something of a hanging judge. Confessions, they don't mean diddly to Justice Hartley." He shook his head a little sadly. "I don't give much chance for that boy back there."

A wry smile. "No. I think you're probably right."

Deep in thought, Cole stepped outside. He'd need to return to the bank, the scene of the crime, and asked some questions. Most especially, he needed to talk to the manager.

CHAPTER TWELVE

"That's serious gunfire," Norton said. "Perhaps we should turn away and make our way to Bethlehem?"

"We do, and they'll hang you as soon as they see you."

"They won't recognize me."

"If your story is true, they'll remember you for the rest of their lives."

"I was wearing my bandana over my face."

"Is that so?"

He smirked. "It's a sort of disguise."

She studied the film of sweat covering his brow, the chalky whiteness of his face, his eyes so dull. "I'm not sure you'll make it to Bethlehem. We need to get you fixed now!"

"I'll make it." He shivered beneath the thick coat draped around him.

Several shots rang out. Cathy leaned forward, narrowing her eyes. She thought she saw some distant puffs of smoke, but she couldn't be sure. "We'll go in from the other direction. I know Doc Farlow's place, so we can go straight to him. Whatever is happening down there, we can ignore it."

"What if it's them? The rest of the gang, helping Jonas with getting himself fixed?"

"If it is, they could all be dead after all that gunfire."

He cocked his head. Silence settled over the cluster of broken and decrepit buildings. "It seems to have finished. Maybe whatever was happening has ended."

"So you see, no need to be a-worrying."

"But I am," he said, pulling the coat tight around him. "If it is Jonas down there and he catches sight of me, I'm dead. Maybe you too. If some other bunch has shot up the gang, they must be as mean as rattlers. Could be they are even more dangerous than Jonas and the rest of the boys."

"Well, there's only one way to find out," and she flicked the reins and edged the buggy in a westerly direction in order to enter the little town from the opposite side.

She hitched the buggy to a sagging tree and jumped down. She checked the Henry.

"You've got to be careful," he said in a croaking whisper.

"I will. You just sit and try and keep yourself warm." She gave him what she hoped was a reassuring smile and shuffled away.

"Don't take the rifle. Leave it with me."

"You said you weren't up to shootin'."

Norton shrugged. "If they see you with that, they'll shoot first and ask questions after you're dead in the ground."

Considering his words for no more than two seconds, she nodded and gave him the Henry. She forced a smile then turned to go.

Norton worried her. She knew he was close to collapse, and it was vital she got him to Farlow's as quickly as possible. Whatever was playing out in the main street had to be ignored as far as possible. No point in tangling herself up in other people's problems. She had plenty of her own. There was no denying the thoughts and feelings racing around inside. Her place needed a man, a good dependable man. Not like Jude and his womanizing, but an upright one, able to stay and help her with the spread, especially now that winter was coming on. Jude always hated the winter, and when they were snowed in, Jude stomped around the cabin like an angry bear. Norton didn't strike her as being like that. Regardless of the crimes he had involved himself with, she cared little about his past and was prepared to give him the benefit of the doubt. Whether Norton was his real name or not, it suited him, and when he was fixed, she'd give him her proposal.

Something moved ahead of her and she ducked out of sight. There were voices, some muffled, but one in particular raised high, "String 'em up, boys!"

She shuddered at the thought, took in a large breath, and edged forward, keeping herself close to the wall of the building beside her.

A gasp almost escaped from her mouth when she saw the broken steps leading up to Doc Farlow's place. In disbelief, she stood and gaped and, almost as if in a dream, she stepped away from the wall into full view of anyone watching and stared up to the top of the shattered staircase.

"Well, well, what have we here?"

The voice, mixed between amusement and surprise, brought her to her senses and, snapping her head around, she saw an elderly looking man in a black tailcoat, leering at her. She thought she recognized him but couldn't be sure, until he moved closer, the leer growing wider with every step.

"Ed Rollins," she said.

He pulled up sharp, frowning. "Do I know you, missie?"

"You knew my husband, Jude." His frown deepened. "Jude Courtauld."

Slowly his face cleared, memory stirring. "Ah, yes, Jude.

You're his …? Well, well, Jude Courtauld. He never mentioned you, or if he did, he never said how pretty you are." He looked back at his men trussing up the remnants of the others, some badly wounded by the look of them. "I'm in the middle of something right now, Miss Courtauld." He turned to her again. "It won't take more than a few minutes, then we can talk."

"I came here to see Doc Farlow."

"Did you now? Well …" Laughing, he shot a glance to the top of the broken stairs. "He's somewhat indisposed at the moment, but I'm sure we can fix it. Are you sick?"

"No, but a friend of mine is."

"Oh, I see. Like I said, let me finish my business, and I'll be right with you."

"What does this *business* consist of, Mr Rollins?"

"It's business that is no concern of yours, Miss. Now, if you'll excuse me."

He doffed his hat and swung away, with something of a jaunt to his step.

Catherine melted into the shadows. The cold was penetrating her overcoat, pinching her skin, and she knew time was pressing. Another glance to Farlow's door brought her only a deepening sense of gloom.

CHAPTER THIRTEEN

"They could be the men we're after – the bank robbers," said Roose, studying the goings-on at the end of the main street.

"Could be," said Coltrane, "but could just as well be not."

"Only one way to find out," said Roose and went to kick his horse forwards.

"Hold on, Sheriff," cut in Knott. "This looks serious, and I can see one or two of 'em down on the ground."

"There's gonna be a-hangin'," said Philips.

"They can't hang those men," said Roose. "They is our men! It's my duty to take 'em back to Bethlehem for trial."

"Shoot, Sheriff," said Coltrane, "dead or alive is what it always says on them reward posters. What difference does it make who it is who does the killing?"

"Our men, you say," put in Knott. "They ain't *my* men. Let 'em hang is what I say."

"I don't believe I've ever rode with such a sorry bunch of whining old women as you!" Roose stared meaningfully towards Brown Owl. "Looks like it's you and me."

The scout grunted, pulled out his Colt and checked its load.

Coltrane looked anxiously from one of his companions to the next. "What are you aimin' on doin', Sheriff?"

"Something you boys would *never* be able to do!"

Roose pulled out the Colt Cavalry from its holster, nodded towards Brown Owl, and set off, kicking his horse hard, breaking into a full charge, with Brown Owl whooping and hollering close behind.

The others stared in disbelief for a few moments before they too, albeit reluctantly and not so fast, spurred their mounts to follow Roose and the scout.

———

They had the three men's wrists lashed behind them when Rollins emerged from the side street, chuckling to himself. His amusement, if that was what it was, soon disappeared when he caught sight of five riders bearing down on them all from the far end of the street. Frozen with indecision, it took him too long to call out to his men. Even as they turned, the riders were amongst them.

Rollins did his best to take some cover. He fanned his handgun as he went to his right, but the first bullet hit him in the back of the leg. He fell to his knees, cursing loudly. As he twisted himself around, clouds of dust obscured what was going on around him. Guns barked, men screamed and horses were out of control. In the swirling nightmare of confusion and blood, Rollins received another bullet in the throat. He fell, gurgling out his last few moments in the dirt.

Sterling Roose managed to control his frenzied horse as it reared up, threatening to unsaddle him. A man, shooting wildly at him, did not help the situation. Roose managed to put a bullet in him, but not before others shot Brown Owl off the back of his pony.

Battling to keep his emotions in check, Roose snapped his head around. The Indian scout lay on his back, rigid. The unmistakable repose of the dead. Gritting his teeth, Roose turned away just as Knott, handgun blazing, received a wound in the guts. He keeled over, anguish and pain screwing up his face. For a moment, Roose believed he would survive, but two more shots burst his head open in a huge red plume of blood and brains.

All around, men were moving and firing. With little idea of how many adversaries he faced, Roose continued through pure instinct, measuring his shots, doing his utmost to keep himself moving whilst he fired. Little success came his way. When Philips crashed to the ground, writhing in blood and gore, Roose dismounted, rolling across the ground, not caring where his horse might go.

On his knees, he expelled cartridges and fed in new. Through the clouds of dust, he spotted them. Two men, rifles in hand, working the levers as if possessed by some mad, uncontrollable desire to kill. He took his time, knowing he must make every bullet count now. He aimed and shot the first of these men through the head. Standing and moving rapidly to his left, he put three more into the second just as he was about to bring his Winchester to bear.

Deathly quiet fell like a great weight around them. Even the horses seemed shocked into silence. Checking around him, Roose reloaded and waited, senses alert, ready to explode into action once more if necessary.

"Oh dear God!"

He turned to see Coltrane falling to his knees, face in hands, sobbing uncontrollably. Ignoring him, Roose tested each of the bodies with the toe of his boot. Seven in all. Everyone dead.

A high-pitched scream shattered the eerie silence and brought everything back into sharp focus. In the narrow side street, a woman struggled in the arms of a man, a man who had a gun to her head.

"You're gonna let me ride outta here," he said, voice trembling with fear, pushing the barrel hard into the side of the woman's head. She whimpered, but the fight was leaving her as the hopelessness of her situation gradually became clear. "I'm taking her with me, as security."

He edged backwards, and Roose watched, going through his options. He didn't have many. He turned around to try and say something to Coltrane and was transfixed in horror. Coltrane had cut through the cords binding the men's wrists and now they were free, shaking and rubbing their hands. How could Coltrane be so stupid? Had he simply decided, without any serious thought, that these men were not the bank robbers?

As if by a signal, Coltrane's face came up, his eyes locked onto Roose, and a wide grin slowly developed as all around him, the robbers retrieved firearms from the bodies of the dead. One of them, a burly looking Mexican, clamped a hand around Coltrane's shoulder. Roose saw it and knew. Of course, it all made sense. The robbers would have needed an inside man to give them vital knowledge about the bank. And there he was, grinning like a loon, triumph written into every line of his treacherous face.

But Roose had no further time to consider any more options. Another scream from the woman and he turned. The gunshot rang out. A single boom from a weapon of much larger caliber than a handgun. The man holding the woman sort of imploded, his head enveloped by thick blood as it sank deep into his neck. His mouth gaped open in a soundless scream as he slid sideways and crumpled to the ground.

"Come on!" roared a voice from the far end of the street.

A man, a large overcoat draped around his shoulders, stood in front of a small buggy, a smoking Henry rifle in his hands.

Paralyzed with fear, the woman stood staring at the dead man at her feet. She was covered in his blood and flecks of bone and brain. Roose, reacting quickly, sprinted to her, scooped up the dead man's gun, took her around the waist and ran with her towards the buggy. The man at the buggy was aiming the Henry. "Get her on top," he said, "and be quick."

Not pausing to debate any of what the man said, Roose bundled the woman onto the seat as the Henry belched fire once again. He chanced a quick look. The released bank robbers were swarming forwards, including Coltrane, guns drawn, murder in their eyes. Roose had a notion to take the Henry and blow Coltrane's head off, but such an action would have to wait. There simply was no more time. Soon, responding gunfire would hail down upon them all.

Roose clambered up onto the seat. This close, the man with the Henry looked ghastly. It was a tight squeeze, all three of them crushed up together, but Roose took the reins and managed to control the horse, turning the buggy in a tight arc. He thanked every angel and saint there is that the buggy was positioned at the far end of the passage, affording enough room to maneuver it away from their attackers.

The man loosed off two more rounds before several bullets came zinging their way. Head down, Roose urged the horse on with violent swishes of the reins. It broke into a goodly gallop, eating up the distance between themselves and the frustrated, screaming robbers, their revolvers firing uselessly, bullets dropping well short.

CHAPTER FOURTEEN

Cole sat in the bank manager's office, leg twitching, anxious to set off and find out what was happening. Next to him sat two other men, dressed in black tailcoats and matching trousers, hats on their laps, side arms prominent, almost as prominent as the large badges pinned to their lapels. United States Marshals, both looking grim and mean.

"Problem is, Mr Cole," the larger and older of the two marshals was saying, "as the money stolen was government responsibility, it falls to the United States Government to retrieve it."

"By whatever means necessary," interjected the younger man.

"You don't know the territory," said Cole evenly. "How you gonna track any of them?"

"We will employ you, Mr Cole," said the older one. "We will pay you far in excess of what the Army paid you during your time with them."

"A daily rate?"

"Indeed."

"Plus a bonus on completion."

"Completion? What does that mean exactly?"

"When we find 'em and bring 'em back here for trial."

The younger one leaned closer to Cole. "Mr Cole, we will take them to Washington for trial. The government is keen to send out a signal that such excesses will not be tolerated."

"So you see, all we need you to do is find them for us." A slick smile. "But we agree to pay you the bonus."

Cole leaned back in his chair, took out a small canvas pouch from his jacket, and prepared himself a smoke. "I was talking to the only surviving member of the gang," he said. "He told me some things, and I said I'd put in a good word for him."

"Things such as what?"

"If I tell you, I need guarantees that he will be spared the rope."

"You know we can't do that."

"That puts me in a somewhat difficult position. You see, with what that young bank robber told me, it sort of complicates things."

"Then you must tell us."

"Not without an assurance." He rolled up his smoke and lit it. He smiled at the bank manager. "You is a personal friend of Justice Hartley, so I understand."

The bank manager turned a shade of puce. "How do you know that?"

A shrug. "Word gets around. I also know there was an insider working for the robbers, feeding them information about the railroad money, when it was due, how much it was, all of that."

"I don't see how any of this is relevant," said the older marshal.

"Well, listen. When I give my word, I stick with it. I gave that boy assurances, so if I'm gonna accompany you gentlemen, I want your word – and yours," he jabbed a finger at the bank manager, "that the boy is given a fair trial. He played no part in the killing. And, because of the information he has supplied, I believe he deserves a break."

"Preposterous!" spurted the manager.

"I ain't got access to any records," said Cole, ignoring the little man behind the desk, "but you have." He looked at the older marshal. "Send a telegram and find out what you can about a man called Jonas Franklin. He's the new boss of the gang, as the original was shot dead in the bank office."

"Oh dear Lord," said the manager, the memory returning. He got unsteadily to his feet and moved over to a drink cabinet in the corner and, with trembling fingers, poured himself a large whisky.

"A telegram? Yes, I can do that," said the older one.

"Good. As for the insider, I want those guarantees."

"Mr Lister," said the older one, nodding towards the manager. "If you know this Justice Harley—"

"Har*tley*," said Cole.

"Yes. Hartley. Perhaps you can tell the judge that this young man had little to do with the killing."

"He had *nothing* to do with it," said Cole.

The marshal gave the slightest of nods. "So, you will convey that to the judge, Mr Lister. If you could be so kind."

Lister drained his glass. "Very well."

"So, who was the insider?"

"A man called Coltrane."

A squawk and Lister dropped the glass. It shattered across the floor. He looked close to collapse. "He is my assistant! It can't be true."

"Why would he lie?" asked Cole. "Besides, how could the prisoner know that name? Of course it's true, and it makes a good deal of sense. They knew the plan of the bank, how much money there'd be ... Who knows what else. It was Coltrane, no question."

Running a hand through his thinning hair, Lister collapsed into his chair. "Oh my, this is all just too terrible." Shaking his head, he produced a handkerchief and used it to dab his sweating forehead. "He is one of the men who joined Mr Roose's posse."

Now it was Cole's turn to react. He stood up, cigarette forgotten. "Then we have to move, gentlemen. And we have to move now, for I fear my good friend, Sheriff Roose, could be in real danger."

"I'll get the horses ready," said the younger marshal, standing up.

"And I will send that telegram." The older one nodded towards the bank manager. "How much went missing, Mr Lister?"

"Hardly anything at all, apart from the money the men took from the tellers and what the other man in my office managed to grab after he'd shot the others."

"And saved your life."

Lister's eyes held Cole's. "Indeed, yes, Mr Cole. Two saddle bags he had. A matter of perhaps twenty-five thousand dollars, I would estimate."

"That's a fair sum, Mr Lister."

"Yes. But they were bank robbers, after all."

The older marshal got to his feet, shook Lister's hand and motioned for Cole to talk with him outside. Lister watched them go, his eyes moving again to the whisky waiting for him in the drink cabinet.

"Will we need more men?"

"No. We'll be just fine. For all we know, Roose may well have tied everything off for us, unless that Coltrane got to him first."

"Which is a possibility," said the older marshal.

"Yes. It is." Cole gave him a measured look. "If we're to ride, I'd prefer to know your name rather than call you marshal."

"Whit. My associate is Deputy Marshal Simpson." He looked at the sky, barely able to contain a shiver. "It's cold, Mr Cole. Will we need extra provisions – blankets, perhaps?"

"And coats. It'll be especially cold at night now that the weather is closing in. Snow is in the air."

"But we won't be on the trail for long, surely?"

"Depends."

"Very well. I shall instruct Simpson to purchase what we need."

"You have rifles?"

"Winchesters."

"Fair enough. I'll meet you in the saloon, but please don't be long."

Cole stepped down into the street, untied his horse from the hitching rail, and walked down to the saloon, aware of Whit's eyes boring into his back but fending off the urge to check. At the saloon, he went straight to the bar and ordered a single whisky then asked for a flask to be filled up. "Gonna be cold," he said by way of explanation.

"I thought you'd retired, Mr Cole," said the bartender.

"So did I," said Cole, finishing off his drink. "So did I."

CHAPTER FIFTEEN

They managed to repair the steps as best they could. Timber seemed to be in short supply, but they ripped off several planks from an old, near-collapsed barn and fashioned them to fit the gaps. Doc Farlow watched them from the top, shaking his head. Beside him stood Maisie, dressed only in her finest Basque, herring-bone ribbed sides accentuating her full figure. She laughed, but could not keep the admiration from her voice when she said, "I do like a man who indulges in manual labor!"

Dragging a forearm across his brow, Coltrane smiled towards her. "And I do like the way you are looking, Miss."

"Name's Maisie."

Her smile grew wider.

"Mine's Jeremiah. Jeremiah Coltrane. It's good to meet you."

"Hey, gringo," spat Cruces, breathing hard. "We need to get this done if the Doc is to fix us." His wound was not healing and oozed a sickening yellow fluid. On the ground, some feet away, lay Jonas. They'd propped him against the wall of the closed-down bordello, and he too looked grim, face swathed in sweat, eyes rolling around. He was conscious but if he was aware of his surroundings, he did not inform anyone, the only sound coming from his slack mouth a long, drawn-out moan every now and then.

By the time they had managed to create a workable set of steps, Doc Farlow could slowly make his way down, although he hesitated at every creak and groan.

"Fix him first," said Cruces, pointing at Jonas as the Doc finally stepped onto the ground.

"You don't look too good yourself," said Farlow. "Boys, help these men to the saloon, gather together some tables and lay 'em both down. Then get lots of boiling water and torn up sheets. Hurry now, time is pressing, and these boys need tending to."

It took them some time. Cruces tried to walk but collapsed after only two steps. Maisie helped, taking the Mexican by the feet whilst Coltrane and Farlow took one of his arms each. Behind them, Len and Channi struggled with Jonas.

Making the saloon, they carried out Farlow's instructions and pressed together several tables and laid the wounded men on top of them. As the Doc retreated into a back room to organize the water, Coltrane went to the bar and ordered whisky all around. Maisie, fanning herself with the palm of one hand, leaned up next to him. "Hot work."

"Sure is," he said and downed his whisky. He slid a glass towards her. She studied it for a few moments.

"How come a man like you has come to this dead-end town and gunned down old Ed Rollins?"

"Ed Rollins got in the way. We're here to rest up, nothing more."

"And those others, the ones who rode off in that buggy. Who were they?"

"You ask a lot of questions, Miss."

"I told you the name's Maisie, Mr Jeremiah Coltrane." Smiling, she lifted the glass to her lips and took a small sip. "I remember yours. If you were a gentleman, you should remember mine."

"I never said nothin' about being no gentleman."

A smile creased her pretty face. "That's what I was hoping you'd say."

The rear door swung open, and Doc Farlow strode in, determination written on his face. Gone was the drunken old man from only hours before. Here he was, the man he used to be. He levelled his gaze towards Coltrane. "I'll need you and your men to hold down the patients. Maisie, if it's not too much trouble, keep the water coming. I have to wash the wounds, extract the bullets and then dress 'em. It's gonna take time and it's gonna be messy."

Coltrane let out a long low whistle. "I'm glad you're on our side, Doc."

"This is not about sides, it's about saving lives. I may be retired, but I still remember my oath. Now let's get to it!"

And 'get to it' they all did. Farlow worked relentlessly, his body leaking sweat despite the cold drifting in through the saloon doors. The barkeep kept everyone well supplied with whisky, Farlow even using some of it to wash over the gaping holes out of which he'd extracted the bullets. Jonas, by now consumed with fever, screamed and writhed while Cruces, a more resolute and stubborn individual, gritted his death and swallowed down the pain.

It took over three hours to get the two men patched up. Jonas was already unconscious. Cruces, drowned in alcohol, mumbled incoherently. At least they were both alive. At least, if they were lucky enough to get through the night, they could ride again.

CHAPTER SIXTEEN

The same could not be said for Norton.

Slowing the buggy down to a steady walk, Roose steered it under the cover of low trees clustered around jagged rocks and smooth boulders. Jumping down, he stretched out his back before taking a look at the wounded Norton. The man's head was lolling on his chest, a trail of saliva mingled with blood drooling from the corner of his mouth. Lifting the man's head by the chin, Roose sucked in a breath. "Wish you'd been able to get him to the Doc's. He's bad, miss. Very bad."

She was sobbing, face in hands. "It's my fault," she said. "I should have tended to him better back at home, but I insisted on him goin' to the Doc's. One of the wounds was festering, and I didn't have the means ..." She looked across at the stricken Norton and released a long, shuddering breath. "He's gonna die, isn't he?"

"Maybe," said Roose. "Maybe not. I've seen plenty of men with wounds this bad, some a lot worse, and they pulled through. He's strong and he's young, but we do need to get that bullet out."

"I tried, honest I did. But I think I only managed to get a piece of it, it was so deep."

"That's what's causing the infection, I reckon. Thankfully, he's unconscious now, so we can give it a try. Help me get him down."

The ground was broken, dry and hard. Cathy tried to make the best of it by rolling out an old blanket. Then she helped Roose carry Norton to the most comfortable spot amongst the trees. Breathing hard, Roose stepped back and studied the young man. "He's one of them, isn't he?" He turned to her, her smooth face creased into a frown. "One of the bank robbers we were hunting."

"Yes," she said immediately before turning away, eyes downcast. "I found him close to my home. He was shot. I managed to get him back, tended to him as best I could, but it wasn't enough."

"He told you what he'd done?"

"He told me the story, yes. I'm not sure he did such bad things, mister. He told me he saved the manager of the bank. Is that true?"

"I'm not sure. All I know is that they are a murdering bunch of desperadoes, and now they done more killing. Including my friend. I can't let that lie." He took a deep breath. "But he did help us back there. I won't forget that, either."

They stood staring at one another for a long time, neither speaking, an understanding of sorts passing between them. Roose saw her as a gentle, forgiving woman possessed of real charm. What she was doing living out in the wilderness all alone was beyond him. The fact she'd cared for Norton suggested to him she was needy, desperate to have someone in her life. Perhaps for the first time, he thought. Perhaps, as so many settlers had discovered, starvation and sickness were never far away in this hard, unforgiving land. "Forgive me, ma'am," he said at last, "you have no family?"

Blinking a few times, she opened and closed her mouth several times as if she struggled to find an appropriate response. "I don't see what that has got to do with anything," she said at last.

Roose held up his hand. "Apologies, I did not mean to intrude. It just strikes me as unusual for a woman like yourself to be living a life out here all on your ownsome."

"I don't have much choice."

"And then to get yourself involved in all of this ..."

"I told you, my home is some way off. I found Mr Norton almost dead, and he told me those responsible were the same ones back at the town. My intention was to take Mr Norton to Doc Farlow's, to fix him up." She blew out a forceful sigh. "If you must know, my husband died not so long ago. Fever took him. We were not blessed with children, so I live alone."

"Dangerous."

"I have managed to survive." Her eyes hardened. "Despite being a woman."

"Ma'am," he now held up both hands in surrender, "like I say, I do not wish to cause offence."

"No, well, that's as may be, but now I think we must do our best for Mr Norton before the night draws in."

"Indeed," he said, reached under the back of his coat, and produced a heavy-bladed knife, its keen edge glinting in the thin sun of the late afternoon. "Have you any water?"

"I have two flasks in the buggy."

"And we'll need something to bandage him up with."

"I'll use my petticoat."

With the heat rising to his face, Roose nodded and turned away. "I'll do my best, but get ready to help me. If he wakes, you'll need to hold him."

"I'm prepared to do everything I can."

And Roose could see by the determined look on her face how truthful her words were.

Sometime later, with the sun dipping below the horizon, Cathy finished securing Norton's bandages while Roose sat with his back against a nearby tree, smoking. Having discarded his jacket, his white shirt drenched in sweat, he gazed into nothingness, lost in his thoughts. The Bowie knife lay next to him, still red with Norton's blood. He'd worked as fast and as carefully as he could, finally managing to dig the rest of the bullet out. The wound stank, worse than anything he could remember, and he felt certain, despite his earlier reassurances, that Norton would not last the night. But he'd done all that he could.

Cathy rocked back on her heels and gave a grunt of satisfaction. "He's sleeping, thank the Lord."

"That's the best thing for him. All we can do now is wait."

"He drifted into fever when I first tended to him. He's weak. I'm fearful for his chances."

"Try not to worry. We can only see what the morning will bring."

A faint smile played around her mouth. "Thank you, mister. I appreciate your help."

"The name's Roose. I'm sheriff of Bethlehem."

"Oh my! I did not realize."

"No reason why you should. I can't recall ever seeing you in town myself."

"I live some distance out of town, Sheriff, as I said."

"Yeah, on your own."

"I manage."

"You said that too." He nodded towards Norton. "Could be you've found someone to ease the burden."

"What do you mean by that?"

"Nothing." He studied the glowing end of his cigarette. "We need to get some rest. We'll start out early, but I'm fearful those desperadoes will cut us off before we make it back to town."

"They know where I live. They could figure we might head for there."

"Well, we have to try and make it to one of them. Either town or your place."

"There is somewhere else, Sheriff. I've been thinking on it. About halfway between the two. The smallholding of a friend of mine name of Larry Grimes. They'll never think of looking there. We could rest there, and Larry could ride into town and get help."

Roose considered her words and could see nothing wrong with the plan.

"Then that is where we'll go," he said, stubbed out his smoke, pulled his hat down over his eyes and drifted into sleep.

CHAPTER SEVENTEEN

The two marshals sat astride their horses, both men swathed in thick buffalo coats, those parts of their faces not covered by scarves were blue with cold. They had slept fitfully, forever turning and stretching, trying their best to find some form of comfort to help them rest. The cold bit deep into their bones, the ground was iron hard and sleep avoided them. They finally managed a few hours and woke to the smell of freshly brewed coffee made by Cole, who seemed rested and fresh.

They headed off not long after but soon Cole signaled for them to stop. Jumping down, on all fours, Cole searched the ground, blew out his cheeks, and stood up. "It's confusing," he said at long last.

"What is?"

"The number of tracks. Quite a few horses have passed this way, but these here," he waved his hand vaguely over some broken ground to his right, "are those of a pony, so Brown Owl was among 'em."

"How in the name of creation can you tell that?" asked the younger man.

"What did you say your name was?"

"Simpson."

"Well, Mr Simpson, I've been tracking for the Army since before the War." He stared out across the plain to the distant horizon, lost in his thoughts for a moment. "Fought Comanch, Apache, and Arapaho. I stood and watched that crazy procession of soldiers, women, bands, and house building materials snaking out of Fort Kearny back in sixty-six. They said they didn't need no scouts as the Platte Road leading to the Bozeman Trail was well known. So I stayed behind and when the news came through later in the year of what had happened, I felt lower than at any other time in my life. The Sioux, they called it 'The Battle of the One Hundred Slain,' and that was precisely what it was." He heaved in a breath. "So yeah, after that, I sort of took stock, questioned my usefulness, but then more trouble broke out with Comanch and I found my days filled with tracking 'em and killing 'em. Many broke out from the reservations. A lot of Kiowa too. They was bad times, Mr Deputy Marshal but it was a job I did and I retired from it. Until now. And that's how I know."

He hauled himself up onto the back of his horse and pointed in a north-westerly direction. "They are headed that way. I'm not sure what is out there. As far as I know, it is open, barren land with very few settlements. Almost all the gold has been mined out and those towns which prospered are now dead and forgotten. Either way, we proceed with caution. Sterling has gone after 'em, with Brown Owl, as good a tracker as any. But those men, the bank robbers, they is cold and ruthless. I warned Sterling, but he is an obstinate man. I just hope in the good Lord that he is well." He pulled out his tobacco pouch and proceeded to prepare himself a cigarette. "A well-used trail passes through not so far away. It's going to be simple from here on in. We still need to be alert, though, so keep your wits about you."

Clicking his tongue, he gently urged his horse forward as he lit up his smoke, the two marshals falling in behind, Cole's words bringing a sullen silence to them all.

CHAPTER EIGHTEEN

C ruces was awake, sitting in a high-backed chair, sipping whisky. His sunken cheeks and dull eyes were the only indications of the trauma he'd been through, but he was strong. Coltrane, watching the Mexican from where he sat at another table with Maisie beside him, knew Cruces would be well enough to ride soon.

Through the bat-wing doors came Doc Farlow, stinking of booze, reeling across to the counter, pummeling it with his fists and demanding another drink. The barkeep, a man by the name of Sefton, shook his head, wiping the counter surface for something to do. "You've had enough, Doc."

"To hell with that!" spat the old medic. "My money is as good as anyone's, now give me a drink."

"No."

Farlow swung a wild, loping punch, which Sefton easily dodged. He caught the old man's wrist, twisted it viciously, turned him around, and shoved him across the room. Farlow crashed against Coltrane's table and slumped to the ground.

Jumping to her feet, Maisie put her hands on her hips and

glared at him. "Doc, you is a disgrace! Go and get yourself a bath and sober up!"

Muttering a mouthful of abuse, Farlow used the palms of his hands to push himself up. "You know what you can do, don't you, Maisie?" He glared at her through bleary, bloodshot eyes. "What we had was something special, now you've gone and bunked up with this piece of rat filth!"

"Now hold on," said Coltrane, a dangerous tone creeping into his voice. "We're all mighty grateful for what you've done for Cruces and Jonas, but you have no need to talk like that. Who Masie wants to be with is up to her, I reckon."

"She's mine," said Farlow, getting to his feet. He swayed from side to side, legs like rubber, his mouth drooling through slack lips. "You hear me? Mine!"

Without any warning, Maisie rammed a straight left into the old man's nose. Squealing, he staggered backwards, hands clamped to his face, the blood leaking between his fingers. She took two steps towards him and swung her knee into his groin and felled him with a left cross that would have graced any prize-fighter's repertoire.

Coltrane whistled, and Cruces burst into laughter, an outburst that soon turned to a groan of real, biting pain. Clutching his leg, he doubled up, panting, "Oh *Santa Maria*, I do not need this sort of entertainment!" He looked up. "It was good fun, but it hurts."

"Why you so hard on him, Maisie?" It was Sefton, coming from around the counter, stooping down and cradling Farlow's head. "Thought you and him had something going?"

"Sef, apart from you, he was the only man here who could still stand, let alone anything else." A sheepish smile spread across her lovely mouth. She turned to Coltrane. "Until I got myself a better offer."

They all laughed as Coltrane took Maisie by the hand and led her to one of the rooms upstairs.

. . .

Afterwards, they both lay beneath the covers, Coltrane smoking, Maisie staring into space. Eventually, she turned into him. He looped one arm around her shoulders, flicking his cigarette across the floor.

"What are your plans?" she asked, voice thick with sleep.

"Difficult to say."

"Try."

He strained his neck to turn to her. "You sure do like asking questions."

"And you sure do not like answering 'em."

He laughed. "True. Comes with my suspicious nature. It's what's kept me alive all these years."

"But you ain't like the rest. The way you dress. You don't carry no gun. I don't see you as a bank robber."

"That's 'cause I ain't. I was the 'inside man' if you wanna put it that way. I'd met Seagrams years ago, and we got to thinking how we could get ahead in this life, make some money. Now he is dead, and I'm left with the remnants of his gang. But you're right, I ain't no bank robber or gunslinger, unlike Cruces and Jonas."

"Jonas. He's the other wounded one, the one that's real bad."

"He's 'real bad' in more ways than you can think! Once he wakes up and his strength is restored, he ain't gonna take too kindly to what has happened."

She propped herself up on one elbow, running the finger of her other hand through the tight, curly hairs of his chest. "What you think he'll do?"

"Blow his top." He chuckled. "We ain't got no money from that bank raid. Norton, he shot Seagrams *and* Jonas. Any money we got was nothing but a few dollars and cents. It's all gone, and Jonas will be itchin' to get more. Once he knows Norton is alive, he'll wanna track him down and kill him. That woman and sheriff who helped him too."

"That ain't gonna make you any more money."

"True, but Jonas is not one to argue with. What he says will happen, will happen."

"What if you show him you've managed to make some money? Maybe that'll calm him down, then ..." She smiled. "I'll not mix my words. I want us to head off to California, start again. You know that."

"Without money, it ain't gonna be possible."

"Which is what I been thinking about. I have an idea."

"Oh really?" He arched a single eyebrow. "What, in this broken-down old town, there's bank filled to the rooftop with gold? Is that it?"

"Not quite. This town was prosperous once and the stage ran right through it. Even though the town is almost dead, the stage still comes through, and it's due in two days."

"A stage? How is that gonna help us?"

"Because this one comes from Denver. It's the main line down to Santa Fe. It's stuffed with money. You could rob it just outside town, split the money, and you and me head off west. What do you think?"

"Sounds easy."

"It is. "

Coltrane untangled his arm, swung his legs from beneath the covers, and sat on the edge of the bed thinking. "This is genuine?"

"Absolutely." She reached over and massaged his neck. "We could be in California, looking for a place to buy within two weeks."

"How come you haven't done this before?"

"What, who with? Doc and Sefton? Rollins was not inter-ested. In fact, his boys used to ride with the stage as a sort of protection, for which the company paid him handsomely. No, there's never been anyone here I could share my dreams with." She nuzzled into his neck. "Until you came along."

A buzz ran through him and he turned, taking her in his arms, kissing her passionately. "I'll tell the others. Two days you say?"

"It normally gets here around mid-afternoon. They then stay the night to rest the horses. If you ambushed 'em out on the prairie, they wouldn't stand a chance."

"It's guarded, you say?"

"Now that Rollins and his men are dead, there's nobody, except the shotgun rider. Your boys will have no trouble. Then we'll all be rich."

He held her close to him, kissing her cheeks and mouth. "Where have you been all my life?"

"Right here. Waitin'."

Laughing, they both fell back into the bed.

CHAPTER NINETEEN

Somewhere, a rooster made its presence clear as the little buggy trundled into the front yard of Larry Grime's home. A somewhat shambolic building with ill-fitting window casements, warped and roughly shaped wall panels, and a door which appeared to be about to collapse, it seemed to be the product of an unskilled carpenter. Its roof sagged under the weight of a huge bird's nest. When Roose brought the buggy to a halt, he spent a few moments gazing at the building in disbelief. "Is this it?" he asked.

"As far as I know," said Cathy, jumping down from the seat. "I've never been here before, but he's always talking about it."

"You mean he wants people to know he lives in ... *this*?"

"Oh, I think he's mighty proud that he built it all by himself."

Roose pushed his hat back from his forehead. "Built is not the word I'd use, if I'm honest."

"Well, try and not mention that to Larry. He is a man of quiet disposition who takes things very seriously – and to heart."

She crossed over towards the porch steps, pausing for a moment before she placed one tentative foot after the other. Roose watched her and smiled. She was a captivating woman, tussled hair and eyes that danced in a slim, smooth face. How does a woman like that manage to keep herself all alone in this land, he wondered. There had to be a queue a mile long of suitors just itching for a chance to share their lives with her. In another life, he might just join them!

A groan beside him jolted him back to the present. Norton's head slumped onto his chest. His breathing was ragged, the man's shirt front spotted with blood dripping from his mouth. If the poison had infiltrated his blood, Roose knew the man's chances were slim. He'd seen it before, many times. An army doctor told him how medical professors over in England had discovered why people died from wounds in the arms and legs. It was all to do with blood poisoning. He didn't begin to understand it, but he saw the sense in it, how a grown bull of a man, shot in the thigh, could be taken from the field, dressed, cared for, and die three days later in writhing agony. He remembered old Bert Howel, shot in the shoulder by a Shoshone arrow, how he tendered to him, and the following day, there Bert was, covered in sweat, screaming like a demon from the bowels of hell and dying, right before Roose's eyes. It was an image seared into his brain. Old Bert was a good man, a darn good tracker too. Learned his craft from the Kiowa boys who worked for the Army. Life and death. This land never gave you an inch. Not one of us.

"Mr Roose?"

Roose snapped his head around to find himself staring at a tall, gaunt man with a shock of red hair, friendly green eyes creased up in a smile, and an outthrust right hand. "I'm Larry Grimes, pleased to meet you." Roose took his hand and shook it, impressed by the strong grip. "I recognize you as

Bethlehem's sheriff, but I do not think we have been properly introduced."

"It's good to meet you, Mr Grimes. Now, if you could, please help me get this fella down before he falls down."

Without a word, Grimes did as asked. Together, they took Norton into the lop-sided edifice Grimes called home. It was something of a struggle for Grimes, as Roose noticed. The man's limp seemed to worsen with every step. It took them both just under ten minutes to settle Norton into a bed in the second bedroom. Roose stripped and bathed him. Cathy then changed his bandages. Grimes studied everything from the doorway, voice sounding serious when he said, "He don't look too good, nor does that wound smell too good either."

"We need to wash it out again," said Roose. "Have you any whisky?"

"About half a bottle. But we'll need more than that. More than clean water and bandages too. We need help – medical help."

"Larry," said Cathy, taking him by the arm and moving him a little away from the bed. "We already been to Doc Farlow."

"Farlow? Dear Lord, Cathy that man hasn't practiced in years. He's a drunk and a fool to boot. Why didn't you go to Doc Henson over in Bethlehem?"

She took a breath, turning to Roose for some support. The sheriff gave a simple nod.

"It's a complicated story, Larry. Have you a mind to listen?"

"I sure have. I want to know what's going on."

"All right, then I'll tell it."

And so Grimes listened to what Cathy had to say. Roose kept himself occupied with Norton, wiping his fevered brow with a cloth, with one ear listening to the details of the story so that he too could have a better understanding.

When she'd finished, Cathy released a long, low sigh. The re-telling seemed to have taken a lot out of her and she moved over to a small wicker chair that sat in the corner. She lowered herself into it. "Things happened so fast," she said to nobody in particular. "One moment I was out in the field, tending my vegetables, the next I'm up to my neck in blood and bullets. You think he'll make it, Mr Roose?"

"Not sure," said Roose, not turning his head, all of his concentration on Norton, concerned with his breathing. "I think whatever is eating through him has got into his lungs. I'm not hopeful unless we can get help."

"I'll go," said Grimes. "It's clear these scoundrels want Cathy and him dead, so they are bound to follow them here. I'm not good with a gun, but I'm assuming you are." He gestured towards the Colt at Roose's waist. "I have a Sharps in the back. It was my papa's from his war days. He served with the cavalry."

"A Sharps would be good," said Roose, looking across to Cathy. "With your Henry, we can hold 'em off for quite some time until Mr Grimes brings help."

"Yes," she said, "I see the sense in it."

"If I go now, I'll make it well before sundown."

"You find a man called Cole. Reuben Cole, you understand? You tell him that I am here and that I need his help."

"Yes, sir. I shall." He smiled and went to a row of hooks on the wall beside Cathy. He pulled down a thick, fur-lined coat and pushed his arms through the sleeves. "You sure you'll be all right here, all on your own?"

"I'm not exactly on my own, Larry." She smiled. "But thanks for asking."

"Cathy, after this is over, maybe we could talk."

"Yes, Larry. That would be good."

"I hope that young fella makes it," and then he was gone. From where she sat, Cathy could watch him limping through the main door into the cold, bright day. "He's a good man," she said. "He never asked me why."

"Why what?"

She turned to Roose. "Why I want Mr Norton to live."

"It's a Christian thing to do, Ma'am."

"Despite him being a robber an' all?"

"Well, from how it's told, he saved the bank manager's life, so I do not believe he is all bad." He sat back, eyes still locked on Norton's feverish brow. "You do know that Mr Grimes is in love with you?"

If he thought this might bring some reaction to her, Roose was wrong. She merely shrugged, a tiny smile developing across her mouth. "I've known that for some time."

Shaking his head, Roose returned to mopping the sweat from Norton's face. "I'll never understand women," he said.

It was later, with Roose sitting out on the porch smoking, the Sharps across his knee that Cathy, with no idea what was occurring many miles away, sat with Norton. He'd rallied a little, the whisky having cleared out a lot of the puss from his wound. What alcohol remained in the bottom of the bottle, he drank, and now his smile was warm and wide. "Thank you," he said, squeezing her hand.

She felt the heat rise up to her jawline, but in the gloom of the tiny room, lit by a single oil lamp in the corner, she knew he could not see. "I didn't do that much. Mr Roose helped more than me, bringing you here."

"I'm not sure where 'here' is."

"A friend's place. He's gone to get help."

"I remember me shooting and I remember seeing Channi's face. Not much else."

"Nothing else matters. You're here and you're safe and soon you will be better."

His smile changed, from warmth to almost a grimace. "I'm not sure that's true, Cathy. I can feel it, deep inside. The poison. I heard what the sheriff said. It's like a snake, writhing around my insides."

"Don't talk that way. Larry will bring back doc Henson and he will—"

"Listen," his grip tightening, "I want to tell you something, whilst my mind is still clear."

"Whatever it is, it can wait. You need to rebuild your strength."

"No, it can't wait. I took money."

Her heart almost stopped. For a moment, she didn't know how to react. "Money? From the bank?"

He nodded. "I filled up two saddle-bags. I put them inside my bedroll, didn't tell any of the others. They was all shook up by what had happened, so no one noticed. Then, when Jonas turned up, I made a run for it, stopping only to bury the money before I made it to the creek by your place. Where they caught me and left me for dead."

Mouth half open, the images his words conjured up ran through her mind. "But you mean … you buried it?"

"Something like ten thousand dollars."

"Ten *thousand* …" Her free hand flew to her mouth. "Oh my. Ten thousand dollars? Are you sure?"

"Well, I could only guess. I didn't have time to count it out carefully. But it's a lot, Cathy. Enough for you to make a good life for yourself."

"A good life for *my*self? What are you saying?"

"I'm saying it's yours. You understand? You get me a piece of paper, and while I am still able, I'll draw a map. It's easy to find, I promise." His face creased up slightly. "Get me a paper, please."

She went out into the main room, rifling through a chest of drawers, finding nothing. In Larry's bedroom, she came across some worn-out old books. She smiled at that, knowing Larry had interests other than running his merchandise store. He was a man of some depth. Even so, the books had the only paper available. She tore out the cover page of one, found a pencil, and returned to Norton. Grunting his thanks, he drew a rough map and handed it across to her. "You follow this route and the money is there in two saddlebags. At least some good will come out of all of this."

"But I don't want to take it ... You're going to get well. Then we can give it back. That would be the right thing to do."

"No. No, it wouldn't. That bank manager, he's a thief. He knew what was going on, I'm sure of it. What he'll do, he'll make a fraudulent claim, telling the bank owners more money was taken than actually was."

"I can't believe that."

"I can. The man's a weasel. Either way, I want you to have that money. You don't tell a living soul, Cathy. You follow my map and you take that money for yourself. You take it and you build yourself a life, a life you can—" He convulsed into a sudden bout of violent coughing. She held him, praying it would stop. When it finally did, he sank back amongst the pillows, exhausted.

Cathy sat, watching him slip into a deep, yet troubled sleep. She sat like that for a long time.

CHAPTER TWENTY

Cruces felt stiff and bad-tempered. Along with the others, he'd been sat hunched up amongst a huge outcrop of rock for what seemed like hours after listening to Coltrane's plan regarding the stage. Reluctantly, they'd ridden out across the range, sullen and silent. Now, however, both Channi and Len were muttering away to themselves, a noise which Cruces found more irritating than squeezing in between the rocks. "Can't you two shut up?" he said at last, the pain in his leg growing worse by the second. Something wasn't right, and he suspected Farlow hadn't done as good a job as the old Doc had said.

"How do we know this is genuine?" asked Channi at last.

"Yeah," put in Len. "Who told Coltrane about this? His new woman? How do we know she is telling the truth?"

"We don't," said Channi. "And how come Coltrane ain't out here with us?"

"He's with that woman, that's why. He ain't left her bed since he first laid eyes on her!"

They both burst out laughing. Cruces watched them but did not join in. He was tired and his leg hurt like sin. Sucking in his breath through clenched teeth, he thought he heard something. He snapped, "Quiet!" and then strained to listen.

The others fell silent.

Senses alert, body tense, Cruces pushed the throbbing in his leg to the back of his mind and peeped out over the top of the rock behind which he sat. The stage, nothing more than a spec on the horizon, was on its way, great clouds of dust thrown up in its wake. "It's coming," he said and pulled out his gun to check the load. "Get ready."

The others did so without argument, repeating Cruces' actions. A new nervousness spread over them, an urgency to get this over and done with. Cruces steadied his breathing and reached across for the Winchester propped against the rock. He worked the lever. "Get ready to run out as soon as I shoot the guard."

"Any outriders?"

"None that I can see. It must be true what Maisie said about Rollins. All his men are either dead or have gone off to find work elsewhere." He carefully rested the Winchester on top of the rock and squinted along the barrel. "I'm not too good with this, boys, so get ready."

"Now he tells us," muttered Len.

"You use it, Len," said Channi, "you're the best of us."

"I can do it," snarled Cruces, one eye closed as he focused his aim. "I just gotta ..."

The stagecoach came inexorably on, those on board unaware of what was about to be unleashed.

They didn't have long to wait.

Cruces eased off the first round.

The bullet sailed harmlessly over the head of the shotgun guard, who immediately shouted out. The driver hauled back on the team of horses, slowing them. "No," yelled the guard, "get 'em moving faster! Faster, I say!"

A second bullet went hopelessly wide. A bead of sweat

dripped from Cruces' eyebrow into his eye. Cursing, Cruces worked the lever and pumped out four more rounds in quick succession, none of which hit their intended mark.

In a blur, Len snatched the Winchester from Cruces' hands and stood up, taking careful aim.

The driver, panicking, cracked the whip, and the horses broke into a wild gallop.

Len fired, and the bullet hit the guard in the chest, hurling him from the buckboard to the ground.

"Ah hell, Cruces," spat Channi, jumping to his feet, "this is turning into a mighty mess!"

He ran out into the open without a pause, firing off his gun into the air as the stagecoach bore down on him. Meanwhile, Len busily loaded up the Winchester. Cruces sat, staring into nothing, both hands shaking uncontrollably. Ignoring him, Len stepped out beside Channi, put the Winchester stock into his shoulder and yelled, "Hold up, or I'll shoot!"

The driver needed no further encouragement and reined in the horses.

Slowing down, the horses eventually stopped and stood, flanks heaving, eyes wide and wild. The driver, jabbering, threw up both hands and said, "Don't shoot!"

As Channi held onto the reins, doing his best to calm the horses, Len wandered over to the stage. "Everybody out," he said and waved his Colt in the driver's direction. "You, where's the cashbox?"

"On the roof," the driver replied, hands still aloft.

"Throw it down, then you get yourself down here also."

"It's locked!"

"I don't give a damn. Throw it down. I won't ask you again."

Twisting in his seat, the driver crawled onto the roof and loosened the leather straps keeping the cashbox in place. It was square, made from dark green-colored cast-iron, and he struggled to edge it to the side. Sweating, he managed to tip it over the edge and it crashed to the ground with a dull, hollow thump.

Len stepped back as the passengers spilled out. Three men and a woman, all of them terrified, hands up high. "All right," said Len, "empty your pockets of anything of value. Be quick now." He turned his head, "Cruces, get yourself out here, you sorry piece of trash!"

Emerging from behind the rocks, Len could see Cruces had changed. Perhaps it was his failure with the Winchester, perhaps it was the wound in his leg, but there was something not quite right with him.

"Cruces?"

One of them, a small bespectacled man in a dark blue suit, took his chance and ran. He made it all the way to the stricken guard, who was rolling around trying to reach his shotgun.

Len snarled, "This is all I need."

But it was Cruces who reacted. Pulling out his revolver, he strode forward and put two rounds into the fleeing man's back. Then he turned his gun to the guard and shot him clean through the head. Whirling around, he returned to the stage. "Sorry, Len. I messed up."

"No, no, Cruces, you didn't, you just ain't any good with a Winchester is all."

"No, I messed up and I'll put it right." He turned his gun on the remaining passengers. Before any of them realized what was about to happen, he shot them all down dead.

"Ah, Cruces," said Len in a small voice, "there was no need to—"

"There was every need," said Cruces, a shudder running across his shoulders. He broke open his gun and ejected the spent cartridges. He quickly reloaded. "I messed up, and it ain't gonna happen again."

He swung his gun arm towards the driver and shot him, the blast hurling the man through the open passenger door where he hung, half in, half out of the coach. Stepping up to him, Cruces put three more rounds into him.

"Cruces!" said Len, grabbing the Mexican by the shoulder and spinning him around. He hit him back-handed across the face, stunning him. "Cruces, snap out of it!"

"What's going on," said Channi, approaching them, studying the dead bodies littering the ground. "This ain't good."

"It's all fine," said Len, shaking Cruces by the shirt front. "Cruces, are you listening to me?"

It took a few moments and another slap before the Mexican emerged from the nightmare he had fallen into. Blinking, he tugged himself free from Len's grip and wandered away.

"Is he sick or something?" asked Channi, close now to Len.

"I think so. Something ain't right with him. Maybe it was the gunshot wound. I don't know, but he's acting real strange."

Cruces found another clump of boulders and sat down. Taking his time, he unbuckled his belt and slid his pants down to his knees. The wound in his thigh was well wrapped but soaked through with watery blood and a green fluid which looked and smelled ghastly. Gingerly, he undid the bandaging, releasing the pressure from his leg, which brought some relief and allowed him to examine the puckered, swollen wound more closely. Farlow told him he'd fixed it, but Cruces knew the bullet was still in there. When he touched the oozing white flesh around the hole a jolt of pain lanced through him. He looked back towards his companions and, in that moment, made a decision. Throwing the bandage away, he hitched up his pants and returned to them.

"Get the cash box open," he said, "and go through every body, taking what we can. Put everything into your saddle bags."

"And the horses?" asked Channi.

"Let 'em go."

"We ain't got no key for the box," said Len.

Quickly, Cruces shot through the lock with his gun. "We don't need one. Now get it emptied and hurry up!"

Len and Channi exchanged a look.

"I said *hurry up*!"

Scrambling to do as he was told, Len threw back the box lid and whistled. He rummaged through the collection of bundled up dollar bills, gold coins, letters and rolls of parchment. "There's got to be at least a thousand in here," he said, "and maybe a hundred gold coins!"

"Get it all in your saddle bags. We have to be quick. I don't like being out here in the open. Who knows who might come along?"

"Coltrane is gonna be pretty happy when he sees this," said Len. "It'll make up for that bungled bank job, give us all a—"

"We ain't going back to Coltrane."

Both Len and Channi stopped in their tracks. "Eh?" Len shook his head. "What do you mean, Cruces?"

"I mean we are taking that money for ourselves. Coltrane is the one responsible for what happened back at the bank so he can go and rot. We take everything and ride down to Mexico. I know people there and we can rest up, live easy, and plan our next move."

The others stood in stunned silence, Cruces' words ringing out like a funeral knell.

"But what about Jonas?" asked Channi in a quiet voice.

"He'll kill us," said Len.

"He'll never find us," said Cruces, some of his old fire returning. "So we ride and we don't look back. Our time has come, boys. We have a chance to make things right, so let's go."

Reloading his gun, Cruces limped across to his horse and pulled down the saddle bags.

Shaking his head, Channi looked at his friend. "You think this is right, Len?"

"I think it makes sense." He looked again at the stash inside the cashbox. "An awful lot of sense."

CHAPTER TWENTY-ONE

Throwing up a hand, Cole signaled for the others to stop.

"What is it?" asked Whit, reining in his mount beside Cole.

"A rider." He pointed to a distant plume of dust moving across the plain.

Whit reached behind and pulled out a long leather case from inside his bedroll. He hastily unscrewed the top and tipped it. A brass telescope slid out, which he put to his right eye, twisting the barrel to focus in on the rider. "Yes, it's as you say. A single rider, red-headed and coming this way." He collapsed the telescope and dropped it back into its case. "Simpson, go and intercept him, find out who he is and why he's in such a hurry."

"Yes, sir," said Simpson and spurred his horse into a gallop.

"That's a mighty fine piece of equipment," said Cole, nodding to the telescope case, which Whit was already pushing into the bedroll. "Always wanted one but could never afford it."

"They are wonderful things," said Whit. "Made in Switzerland."

"Where?"

"A country in Europe. Never ever been. I bought it from an associate I met back in Kansas City about two years ago."

"An associate?"

Whit chuckled. "Let's just say he wouldn't be needing it for at least ten years."

They fell into silence and waited until Simpson returned with the newcomer, a gaunt man dressed in store-bought clothes and boasting a thick shock of red hair. Bathed in sweat despite the cold, the man's eyes leaped from one to the other, his speech coming fast. "Thank the Lord Almighty you good gentlemen came across me! I've come from my ranch, a small one but home to me, and it was there that Cathy and a sheriff from Bethlehem brought in a young fella suffering terribly from a gunshot wound, worst I ever seen. I think he is gonna die, and that is why I'm riding for all I'm worth to fetch Doc Henson to try and fix him up. But I am fearful it'll be too late because—"

"Hold on, young fella," said Whit with a smile. "You just ease on down. You been riding long?"

"No more than a few hours. My place is only a short ways away, and I could show you it after we get the Doc."

"That won't be necessary," said Whit. "Mr Simpson here has considerable medical knowledge." The young deputy marshal blushed and looked away.

"A sheriff was with them, you say?" asked Cole.

"Yessir, indeed he was. Out of Bethlehem, on the trail of bank robbers is what he said."

"Catch his name?"

"Yessir, as I own a store in Bethlehem. Merchandise store, selling all kinds of—"He stopped when he saw Cole's face.

"Sorry, I'm rambling … Sheriff Roose, of course. The only sheriff we got."

"Lead us back to where you have come," said Cole quickly before he shot Whit a glance. "We need to get there right now."

"Indeed," said Whit. He flicked his horse into a trot and soon all four of them were cutting across the plain towards Grimes' home, Cole forever wondering what he was going to find there.

What they found was a small, ramshackle old cabin with no square corners and a roof that was in imminent danger of collapse. But there was something else. A heavy, depressed atmosphere and a woman sitting on the creaking porch steps, weeping uncontrollably. Behind her in the doorway, smoking, stood Sterling Roose, in his shirt despite the cold and his face grim and strained. It lightened slightly when he saw Cole and the others ride up and dismount.

"Looks like you've got yourself in a mess, Sterling. As usual," said Cole, crossing to his friend. They embraced, Cole unable to keep the relief from his voice. "It's good to see you." He stepped back and saw the worry lines etched so deep into his friend's face. "Where's Brown Owl?"

Roose swallowed. "Dead."

Cole went deathly white. For a moment he lost the ability to speak. "Dead?"

Roose looked down. "We barely got out alive, Cole. If it hadn't been for Norton laying down covering fire, they'd have shot the rest of us down, I reckon."

Cole's eyes slowly turned away and he stood staring into the distance recalling that day, so very long ago, when he'd rescued his good friend Brown Owl from certain death. And how the debt had been repaid many, many times over.

Whit stepped up. "Did I hear you say Norton? He'll be the one who shot the gang leader?"

Roose nodded. "And now he's gone too. Died just an hour or so ago. You are …?"

"U.S. Marshal Damien Whit. This is my deputy, Bradley Simpson. As an attempt was made to seize railroad money held in a secure bank, we are agents of the government, instructed to track down the perpetrators and bring them to justice."

Roose watched Grimes moving over to Cathy and noted the man's limp. Sitting down next to her and holding her close, Roose saw how intimate they were. He continued to watch as he spoke. "Well, there ain't many of 'em left, from what I could tell. They shot up some of the locals before they turned their attention to us." He turned again to the marshal. "I calculate there were four or five of 'em."

"And the town they were at?"

"I'll take you."

Whit grunted. "We'll rest up for a little while until the horses have been fed and watered." He looked towards the sky. "It's gonna snow."

"All the more reason why we should leave as soon as we can," said Cole. "So let's get these animals cared for and move out."

As the law officers moved around in a flurry, Cathy drew in a large breath, wiping the last of her tears with her sleeve. "Oh, Larry," she said, her voice trembling, "what sort of a world is this where all we do is suffer and labor without any just reward?"

"I guess we all came out here because of the promise of a new life, Cathy. An opportunity to grow, to settle down, raise a family."

"You haven't."

"No. Not yet."

"You mean with Florence Caitlin?" She grinned at his shocked expression. "Larry, everybody knows how much you like her."

Shaking his head, unable to conceal his embarrassment, Grimes turned away. "Everybody 'cept Florence herself."

"Well, perhaps you should tell her."

"Tell her? Dear Lord, Cathy, I can't do that!"

They both laughed, but soon Cathy's face crumpled again. "I grew to like Mr Norton. I knew he was with that gang and all, but he did honorable things, Larry. He saved the bank manager's life, and he saved ours too. He was a good man."

"And you was hoping something might come of it?"

"I did my best to make a life of it with Jude, but he was a lying, cheating scoundrel. Yes, I grieved for him, but only because I was alone. When Mr Norton came into my life the way he did, so unexpected, I truly felt the Lord was looking down on me."

"But now you don't think that?"

"Nothing is certain in this world, Larry. And certainly not out here. Yes, there was that promise you mentioned, but when it all goes bad, there is no place to turn, no one to help."

"There's always me, Cathy."

Frowning, she studied him, his face so awkward looking, but expectant also. What did he mean, she wondered. "Well, we're not exactly neighbors, are we?"

"No, but ..." He suddenly stood up, his attention caught by the others unsaddling the horses, rubbing them down, and preparing the feed. "Norton, he ...?"

"He just gave up. The poison got to him in the end. You should have seen it, like green yarn threading through his body. Mr Roose said he'd seen it before. Gangrene he called it. He said once it got into the brain, that was it. Norton would cease to be human." She gasped and broke down again, so unexpectedly that Grimes was left stunned, unable to do anything but watch.

After a few moments, he sat back down beside her, put his arm around her and held her close. Then the storekeeper became the man he'd always hoped he would be, and although his voice rattled with uncertainty, he managed to get out the words he'd longed to say. "Cathy, if you're willing, then we could make a go of this hard life together. My store is doing well and your place, with its possibility to grow vegetables, maybe even crops, then we could—"

"Larry Grimes," she said, sniffing loudly, "is this your idea of a proposal?"

Her bloodshot, black-rimmed eyes peered up towards him and he couldn't help himself in reaching out and wiping away her tears with the back of his hand. "I suppose it is, yes."

She gave a tiny laugh. "Oh, Larry, what a funny man you are."

"Am I?" He couldn't help but sound hurt. "Is that how you see me, Cathy?"

"No, no," she said, taking his hand and holding it, "that's not what I mean." She smiled and sniffed again. "Let's us bury Mr Norton first, then I'll give your words some serious thought."

"You promise?"

Another smile before she leaned forward and kissed his cheek. "Promise."

CHAPTER TWENTY-TWO

They were at crossroads, literally and metaphorically. The old trail slinked down towards the south and, eventually, Mexico. Taking a westerly direction would lead them once more to Jonas and Coltrane. More than once, Cruces had debated within himself how he could broach his decision to the others. He knew they were loyal to Jonas, had ridden with him for years, but what they didn't understand, what they *failed* to understand, was that everything Jonas had ever planned, ever touched, had turned to disaster. The bank robbery almost cost him his life. It had certainly cost the lives of too many of the gang. And Coltrane? His 'insider information' had proved bogus. No, they must now consider themselves, what was best for them. They had money. Enough to start again. He voiced his ideas, and now they sat, the three of them, astride their horses, eyes locked on the trail and the promise of what lay ahead.

"I'm not sure," said Len at last. "Why don't we just ride back to Jonas, tell him your plan, and take it from there."

"I agree," said Channi. Bending one knee over his saddle

pommel, he rolled himself a cigarette. "I don't see the point in making an enemy of Jonas. You know how he can be."

"Jonas is close to death."

"Well," continued Channi, running his tongue along the edge of the paper, "you say that, but you don't know for sure."

"I have to say," put in Len, "the way your leg is swelling up, Cruces, I'd say you were closer to meeting your maker than Jonas is."

"Yeah," chuckled Channi, admiring his rolled cigarette with some pride, "who's to say you'll even make it down to Mexico."

Cruces exploded into action. He grabbed for his gun and loosed off the first shot before it barely cleared the holster. Yelping, Channi flung himself to the ground, rolling over in the dirt, scrambling for some nearby cover. Len, reacting as quickly as he could, put a bullet into Cruces' guts before he too received a bullet from the Mexican. It took him high in the shoulder, right next to his carotid artery. He collapsed backwards, the blood pumping horribly from the terrible wound.

Bent double, Cruces slid from the saddle of his terrified, out-of-control horse, clutching at where Len's bullet had struck him. On his hands and knees, he did his best to crawl away, firing blindly to where he thought Channi might be. But all of his shots went wild. By the time he reached a clump of velvet mesquite, which afforded him some cover, his gun was empty, and he realized, in horror, he had no further cartridges.

Channi, however, did not know this. He watched in despair as the horses galloped off, kicking and bucking. He made a quick calculation and decided to cut across country to return to Haven, tell the others what had happened, then come back and do for Cruces once and for all.

Shooting two speculative shots towards the clump of

mesquite, he set off at a steady trot, thankful for the cold air. If this were summer, he knew he'd be dead from thirst before the day was out.

Waiting until only the silence engulfed him, Cruces staggered to his feet. Len was lying a few feet away on his back, drenched in blood, fingers of his left hand pressed into the bullet wound, but his eyes were wide open, staring into oblivion.

Dead.

Cruces managed to make his way uncertainly to his former friend. He ripped away the dead man's shirt and neckerchief. Fashioning a crude, padded dressing, he pressed it hard against his stomach and pulled his own shirt tight around it. He knew all about gut wounds, so, with his jaw set hard, he turned about and set off the way he had come, directly opposite to Channi.

CHAPTER TWENTY-THREE

"We may need that telescope of yours again, Marshal," said Cole, pulling up his horse as his eyes settled on the dark bundle some way ahead.

Whit did so, pulling in a breath as he turned the focus ring. "It's a man and he's in trouble."

"Another one?" said Simpson. His voice sounded bored, as if he were resigned to yet another delay in capturing the bank robbers.

Snapping the telescope shut, Whit turned to his younger deputy. "We can't leave a man out here to die. We have a duty."

"He could be one of them," said Cole. "Perhaps an argument, a disagreement over plans? Who knows, but a single man being all the way out here on foot is strange to say the least. Let's take a look at him."

Cantering across the expanse of hard, gradually freezing landscape, they circled the desperate man, who continued his utmost to keep moving despite falling down repeatedly.

"He's wounded," said Simpson. "We should leave him."

Grunting, Whit dismounted and bent down to the injured

man. He gently turned him over and hissed when he saw the severity of the man's wound. "It's bad."

"Leave him," repeated Simpson, turning his gaze to the far distance. "We need to get to the town and round 'em up."

"What's eating you, Simpson?" snapped Whit, standing up, brushing off the dirt from his trousers. "You got something else you need to be doing?"

"Not at all, sir, but we were given instructions to apprehend these men and bring them to justice – not nursemaid them back to health."

"All righty," said Whit, "seeing as you are so determined to follow through our instructions—"

"I am indeed, sir."

"Well, you can take this man back to Larry Grimes' home and fix him up yourself."

Simpson's face dropped. "I beg your pardon, sir?"

"He's not gonna make it to the town with us, and he sure as anything can't stay out here, so ... You take him to Grimes, you patch him up and wait for us there. Then, when we return, we will escort the lot of them back to—"

"Bethlehem," interjected Roose quickly. "That's where they'll face justice."

Grumbling under his breath, Whit mounted his horse and pointed to the wounded man. "Get him on your horse, Deputy, and ride back to Grimes. It's barely a couple of hours, so he should make it. What do you reckon, Sheriff?"

Roose shrugged. "A man with a wound like that, I'll give him a day at best."

"Well, there you are," said Whit.

"His leg is bleeding too," said Cole. "He's been shot to pieces."

"And he's Mexican," said Simpson.

"Damn your hide!" snapped Whit. "He's a human being

and you'd do best to remember that, Deputy, or I'll revoke your service right here and right now."

Stunned, Simpson roamed his eyes from one man to the next. Everyone stared back, unrelenting, unforgiving. He would find no allies there.

Allowing his shoulders to droop, Simpson reluctantly dropped from his saddle and helped the wounded man to his feet. A pair of black eyes stared deep into him. "*Gracias,*" was all he said.

Cole helped the deputy put the man onto the horse, then held the reins as Simpson mounted up behind him. He nodded towards the scout and grudgingly turned his horse away and kicked it into a lumbering trot.

"Hope it's for the best," said Cole and hauled himself into his saddle.

"If it wasn't for you, Marshal," said Roose, "I'd have put a bullet in his brain after what he's done."

"As a sheriff," said Whit, "you should know better."

"I'm also a man who has been grievous hurt. I lost some good men to that band of vermin. I'll not be lectured by you or anyone else over what is right or wrong."

"Sterling," said Cole evenly, "he'll swing at the end of a rope soon enough, and you can dance a jig in front of him if it'll make you feel better."

"To hell with you, Cole!"

"Brown Owl was my friend too, don't forget."

Leaning over his saddle, Roose hawked and spat into the dirt. "Let's just get this done." He kicked his horse towards the distant town of Haven.

CHAPTER TWENTY-FOUR

With a good deal of care, treading slowly, planting each step without making any noise, Channi approached the jittery, waiting horse before him. Soothing words came from his mouth, low and slow, "There, there, my lovely ... Hush now ... It's all right ... Shush, there's my love ..." Until, at last, he could reach out and take the reins. The relief rushed out of him, and he pressed his face against the horse's neck, closed his eyes, and almost wept.

He checked the saddle bags, felt his knees buckling, and had to hold onto the stirrup to stop himself from falling. The money was there. Drawing in several deep breaths to calm himself, he drank fitfully from the canteen hanging from the saddle, pulled out the blanket roll, wrapped himself in it, and climbed onto the back of the horse. Patting its neck, he nudged the horse forward and settled himself for the ride back to Haven.

. . .

Less than an hour later, Channi entered the small, crumbling town, immediately spotting Coltrane standing in the doorway of the saloon.

"Well, well," said Coltrane, coming down the broken steps to hold Channi's horse whilst his friend dismounted. "You took your good, sweet time. Where are the others?"

Channi's eyes, red-rimmed with tears of anguish, so Coltrane suspected, could barely hold his own emotions in check. "It was bad. Real bad." He pushed past him and half-ran up the steps, blasting through the batwing doors. Hitching up the horse and taking the heavy saddle-bags, Coltrane slowly followed.

Channi was at the counter, gulping down a beer that the barkeep provided.

From the far corner, Maisie appeared. She looked troubled, shooting a questioning glance towards Coltrane, who merely shrugged.

"What happened, Channi?"

They all turned towards the voice's owner.

Jonas, sitting at a table dealing himself cards, reached for the whisky in front of him and downed it in one. "Fetch me another, Sef."

"Why not just have the bottle?"

A small chuckle. "I need to stay sober – for now." He slammed the glass down onto the tabletop. "Now, get me a fill-up!"

Sefton quickly did as ordered, pouring another whisky into a small glass and taking it to Jonas, who stared at it for a few moments before downing it in one. Smacking his lips, he leaned back in his chair. "Surprised, Channi, to see me looking so sprightly?"

Swinging around with his back to the counter, Channi held the beer glass in one hand while his other hovered close to his gun. "I always knew you was tough, Jonas."

"So where are the others?" asked Coltrane,

Channi's face dropped. "Dead. You never told us they had guards with 'em, Coltrane. Outriders. Darn good ones too, truth be told."

"Truth?" Jonas stuck his thumbs into his waistband. "You better not be lyin', Channi."

"Why would I do that? I'm here, ain't I?"

"Yes you are," said Coltrane, and he dumped the saddle-bags onto the nearest table. "How much?"

"Enough to set us up down Mexico way," said Channi. "That's our best bet now, I reckon."

"Is that so?" said Jonas. "You making all the decisions now, is that it?"

"No, I just think it makes sense."

"Is this your plan, or was it Cruces'?"

"Cruces is dead. Len too. Those outriders shot us all up as soon as we charged in on 'em."

"But you managed to do what was needed?"

Channi jerked his beer glass towards the saddlebags. "Seems that way, don't it!"

Laughing to himself, Jonas rocked his chair forward again and stood up. "Mexico?" He wandered over to the saddlebags and pulled them open. He carefully counted through the paper money and coins.

"We could use it to recoup," said Channi, "before we plan out another job."

"Recoup?" Janus raised an eyebrow. "That's a fancy word, Channi."

"It means rest up, lick our wounds."

"I know what it means." He swung away from the table. "What do you think, Coltrane?"

"You know what I think."

"Tell us again."

"That we go to California. They won't think to look for us there."

"California," said Channi, laughing loudly. "Are you crazy? It'll take us weeks to get there. And what do we do then? Eh? No, Jonas, we gotta head for Mexico. They won't cross the border. We'll be safe."

Rubbing his chin, Jonas went to the bar and eyed the few remaining bottles. "All right, Sef, I'll have that whisky bottle now. In fact, that there Kentucky one will do just fine."

"It *is* the finest, Jonas."

"No arguments then." He grinned and took the proffered bottle. Pulling out the stopper, he savored the aroma and poured himself a glassful. "I shall retire to consider my verdict," he said with a chuckle and made his way back to his table and his cards.

Coltrane looked from Channi to Maisie and sighed.

In one of the bedrooms where once the bar girls had entertained their customers, Doc Farlow lay with his eyes staring at the ceiling. He wasn't seeing anything, however, all of his attention centered on the exchanges down below. So, that was it. Coltrane and Maisie would be setting off to California. How had it come to this? Clenching and unclenching his fists, he did his best to sit upright, but his body ached beyond imagining from where Maisie's blows had thundered into him. Collapsing back down amongst the covers, he gulped in air, closed his eyes, and forced himself to lie still and wait. Every passing minute would make him stronger. And then he knew what he would do.

CHAPTER TWENTY-FIVE

The man stank of sweat and leather, forcing Simpson to screw up his nostrils and turn his face away. Crammed up together on the back of his horse, the deputy found himself wishing he was back in Kansas City with his feet up in a nice, warm office, drinking coffee and not doing much else. Anywhere but here. Cold wind bit deep into the flesh beneath his coat. His ears and nose hurt and his fingers, encased in leather gloves, were numb.

This was as far from the promise made to him when he first volunteered himself for service less than six months before. They said, due to his outstanding character and remarkable pistol skills, he would soon find himself in a Washington post, training others. It was all hogwash, and he felt himself a fool for swallowing it all. Closing his eyes, he tried to rid his mind of images, thoughts, hopes and prayers, and simply allow the animal beneath him to keep plodding on. There really was no other choice.

More than once, the wounded Mexican gave a cry and slid from the laboring horse, hitting the dirt with a painful sounding thud. Each time Simpson would curse, dismount,

115

and struggle to get the big, bulky man back in the saddle. At least the exertions kept the cold at bay. For a few moments, at least.

By the time they reached Grimes' home, Simpson was exhausted. He longed for a hot bath and a good night's sleep, but knew he wouldn't get either.

Miss Courtauld greeted them as they plodded up to the cabin. She held onto the reins as Simpson dismounted then, together with the deputy, helped take the wounded man inside.

Cathy directed them to the same bed where Norton had breathed his last.

Wringing her hands, Cathy stepped back to consider the swarthy, bloodied stranger. "Seems like I should be turning this place into a hospital, Mr Simpson."

"Indeed, Miss Courtauld. I do apologize for all of this, but we found him out on the prairie, and Marshal Whit insisted I bring him here before he is taken back to Bethlehem for trial."

"Well, I don't suppose there is a good deal we can do except make him as comfortable as possible. I have some chicken broth on the stove if you would like some."

"Oh, Miss Courtauld, I would indeed. The cold has developed mightily these past few hours."

"We'll soon be up to our necks in snow, Mr Simpson. I do so wish Mr Roose and Cole are able to return before it becomes impassable."

"They will return, I am certain of it."

"Then let me fetch you that broth. Sit yourself down by the fire, Mr Simpson, and warm-up those bones!"

Simpson watched her go, gave the Mexican a searching look, then went into the main room where he sat in a rocking chair by the fire, warming his palms in front of the flames.

Cathy brought in the broth on a tray, settled it down on

Simpson's knees, then slipped into the small bedroom. As Simpson tried not to slurp, he heard her rummaging around inside the room. On her return, he said, without turning his head, "I believe he is a dangerous man, Miss Courtauld, so please take care when you tend to him."

"I was merely checking his wound. It's bad. Much worse than Mr Norton's, and look what happened to him." She came and stood beside the fire. "This is an unforgiving life, wouldn't you say so, Mr Simpson?"

"I'd say it was hard, unpredictable and surprising ... but I do believe those of us who choose to live in this land can make good from it."

"You could be right." She smiled down at him. "I hope you are."

"This is mighty fine broth, Miss Courtauld."

"Oh, do call me Cathy, please."

Nodding, he put another spoonful of broth into his mouth. "Can I ask where Mr Grimes is?"

"In town, tending to his store. He runs a merchandise store, you know. He sells just about everything, and he is successful. I'm hoping he will be more so."

"He has the good fortune to have set-up in a prosperous town, not like many of those 'ghost' towns which are left to rot right across the Territory." He swallowed down the last portion of broth and sat back, contented. "My, that was good. Mr Grimes is a very lucky fellow, I have to say."

Feeling the heat rise to her face, Cathy swung away. "Oh, now hush with all of that!"

He laughed, passed her the empty bowl and stood up. He stretched. "I may have to go back to meet up with the others."

"But you can't – what about the prisoner?"

"Yes, I will do what I can for him and then stay here until Mr Grimes returns. But prisoner is a good description of him.

I do not know exactly what he has done, or how involved he has been with all of the troubles, but like I said before, any one of that gang are potential killers. I may have to restrain him before I go. Given that, I shall just go and check on him and make sure all is well."

He went over to the tiny bedroom door and eased it open.

Cruces was grateful for what they had done. He knew that without their help he would be dead by now. But he also knew he would never consent to being taken back to face a judge and jury, people who would want him dead before the hearing had barely begun. So he listened carefully to what the man and woman were talking about, looked around the room and found something he could use. Somewhere along the way, as he crossed the wide-open prairie, he'd lost his own and Len's gun. Fate just didn't seem to be on his side, no matter what.

With the old, knobby walking stick he found in the corner in his hand, he managed to shuffle behind the door, cramping up with pain, the bandages packed hard up against his guts already soaked in blood. He knew he didn't have much longer, but if he could force the woman to drive him over to Bethlehem, there might still be a chance for him.

He heard the clatter of spoon against crockery and sucked in a breath, gripping the end of the walking stick as hard as he could.

The door swung open and in stepped the big, tall deputy marshal, who seemed taken aback by the sight of the empty bed. It was all Cruces needed. He cracked the walking stick hard across the back of the man's head, dropping him to the floor. Quickly, Cruces threw away the stick and reached for the man's gun. His face came up, and for a moment, they locked eyes. But now Cruces had the gun. He stepped back grinning and shot the deputy through the head without a thought.

From the other room came the piercing scream of the woman. Cruces wanted to go after her, but the exertions had cost him. He swayed back to the bed and collapsed onto the edge, wheezing in breaths, struggling to overcome the pain.

She knew what it was, that single, barking eruption from the bedroom. She screamed, the horror of it all so overwhelming. This nightmare was never going to end, she knew that. Racing outside, she ran to the buggy. There was only one thing to do now. Hadn't Jude always told her that in this land, you did not hesitate to do to others what they would do to you?

Throwing back the seat lid, she brought out the Henry, made sure it was loaded, and strode into the cabin.

Alerted to the stomping of shoes upon the floorboards, Cruces managed to get to his feet. He'd compel her to take him to the Doc's in that hellish place they called Bethlehem. There was no choice. He was weak, close to the end, and the only way he was ever going to make good of this, return to Haven, kill Channi, Jonas, and Coltrane and get that money was if he were fixed up good and proper. After that, he would go to Mexico and live out his days in peace and quiet. This life here held nothing but pain and disappointment, and if he could do anything to change things, then he had to—

The door kicked in, and Cruces jerked himself upright. She was there, standing feet slightly apart, a look like something from his worst nightmares etched into her cold, hard features. And the gun. The way she pointed it directly towards him. Surely she wouldn't ...

. . .

Not much later, Cathy brought the horse to the buggy and hitched it up. She buttoned her thick overcoat to the neck and clambered aboard. She settled the Henry beside her and steered the horse out of the front yard, heading towards Bethlehem. Larry would be alarmed at what had happened, but at least now it was over. They could move on. Make all of this something to forget.

But even as she bucked along across the hard, uneven ground, she knew she could never forget that look on the Mexican's face moments before she blew him apart and the first of many tears tumbled down her face.

CHAPTER TWENTY-SIX

The bodies lay black and bloated on the freezing hard ground. Whit, despite being used to seeing dead bodies, turned away and vomited. Roose stood in silence, staring, and Cole, flipping open the lid of the cashbox with his boot, let out a long sigh. "These coyotes belong in the ground, Sterling."

Roose's gaze settled on the woman. Dressed in richly embroidered clothes, her bonnet still delicately positioned on top of her curly, auburn hair, in life she had been remarkably handsome. "I reckon you're right, Cole."

Cole checked the ground, studying the tracks. "They made off quickly, which don't surprise me none. No doubt we'll find the place where they argued and from where that Mexican ran from."

"We ain't got time for that," said Whit, taking a long drink from his canteen. "We know what they did, and it makes it even more pressing that we bring them in." He shook his head. "There was no need to do this to these poor people. We'll give them a decent burial later on."

"Buzzards will be finishing off what they've already started by then," said Roose. "We'll do it now."

"We haven't the time," said Whit. "For all we know, they could have already got clean away."

"I doubt it," said Roose. "These vermin will be counting their money from this haul before setting off anywhere. Besides, they don't know we're coming."

"We can't bury them," insisted Whit. "We haven't the tools, damn it!"

"Then we burn them," said Cole. "We put them into the stagecoach and set it alight. It's better than leaving 'em out here to rot."

"That's not the Christian thing to do," said Whit, pressing fingers into his eyes.

"It's the *decent* thing to do, Marshal," said Roose.

Nodding, Cole looked at the sky. "We have less than an hour of sunlight left."

"That might work to our advantage," said Roose. "Let's get this done."

In less than that hour of dwindling daylight, the stagecoach was engulfed in flames, and the three of them stood, hats off, watching it burn. Whit said some words and then they all mounted their horses and rode slowly towards Haven.

Stopping some way outside the town, the three horsemen gathered their coats around them. The chill wind shivered through what little undergrowth there was. As they waited, the first flurries of snow descended from the rapidly darkening sky. Night was almost upon them, and down in the dip, lights appeared in the few remaining buildings.

"It'll be best if we dismount," said Cole, reaching to pull out his Winchester from its scabbard. He checked the load, then did the same for the Colt Cavalry at his waist, positioned as always for a cross-belly draw.

"We'll take either side of the main street," said Roose, getting down from his horse. "Or should I say, the *only* street. You get to the rear of the saloon, Cole. I think it's a safe bet that's where they'll be, and you can pick 'em off as they try to run off."

"You seem to know the layout pretty well," said Whit.

"There's not much to know. There's really only one street with a couple of narrow passages here and there. As you can still see, even in this feeble light, the town's on its last legs. After we've finished here, I reckon it'll disappear into the dust."

"I've a tendency to think that that is the right and proper thing to happen," said Whit. He swung down from the saddle, from which he brought out a scattergun. He cracked it open and fed in two cartridges from a pouch. Putting the remaining cartridges in his coat pockets, he cradled the gun over the crook of one arm.

"We'll hobble the horses," said Roose, "keep 'em here until it's done."

"Gentlemen," said Whit, "may I remind you that these men are to be apprehended and taken to justice."

"Let's just see how it goes," said Cole and worked the lever of the Winchester. He had the image of the murdered passengers in his mind. And Brown Owl. He let out a prolonged sigh. "Move down real slow. This cold night air will amplify any noise, so tread gently."

"I am in the presence of men who have done this type of thing often," said Whit.

"Too often," said Cole.

"Sometimes," put in Roose with feeling, "not often enough."

. . .

The street was deathly quiet. No sound came from the saloon, although, from where he stood on the opposite side of the street, Roose could clearly see light from a number of oil lamps through the murky, grime-infested window and underneath the batwing doors. He was under the porch of an old, broken-down dry-goods store, which gave him an idea. He gently eased open the door and went inside. Forced to strike several matches, he found what he hoped would prove useful. Setting it up outside, he positioned himself in an advantageous situation, drew his gun, and waited.

Meanwhile, Whit, following the plan they'd worked out as they approached the main street, stepped up onto the board-walk leading to the saloon. He waited, listening for anything from inside. There came the occasional cough, a muttering of voices, the clink of glasses. He could not make out how many people were inside, but he could hazard a guess. Although the original gang had been whittled down, he knew them to be ruthless men. He was not about to take any chances. He gently eased back the twin hammers of the scattergun and took a deep breath to settle himself.

At the rear of the saloon, Cole waited in the shadows. When the firefight broke, he would take down anyone who came running out of the door without any warning. Unless it was Jonas. For Jonas, the situation was personal.

Roose, one eye on Whit, rolled himself a cigarette. He stuck it between his lips, where it remained unlit. For now.

Whit closed his eyes. The last time he'd fired his gun in anger had been in a mining town just west of Abilene. Things were bad, and prospectors were close to losing their patience. They'd been sold a lie, that gold was there, and they'd readily purchased mining rights from an unscrupulous fellow called Timothy Bothwell. Bothwell was nowhere to be found, but when a group of miners shot up the stage and murdered the sheriff, who they believed was in cahoots with Bothwell, the US Marshals were called in. The confrontation didn't last much longer than it took Whit to fire two rounds from his scattergun, wounding several miners. One fellow made the mistake of going for his gun and Whit shot him through the throat. They all gave up after that.

Three years ago and counting. He hoped never again to have to face such violence. Hopes now dashed.

Whit ripped off his neckerchief and dabbed the sweat from his forehead. He stuffed it in his pocket, kicked through the doors, and blew out the first one, then a second large oil lamp, sending out showers of glass. Those inside leaped to their feet, a woman screamed, and Whit drew his revolver and shot out another lamp at the end of the bar. One remained, but he didn't have time to do anything about that. The initial shock had worn off and guns were appearing. Before the bullets started flying, he dipped back outside and slammed himself against the wall.

It all got very confused after that.

CHAPTER TWENTY-SEVEN

A cting quickly, Jonas upturned the table at which he'd
been drinking and loosed off several shots towards the
batwing doors as they flapped shut. He screamed, "Channi,
go take a look outside!"

"No way," said Channi, flat on his stomach, edging
towards a far corner. The one remaining oil lamp gave enough
light for him to find a path to his chosen cover.

"Just take a look under the door, damn it!"

Rolling over onto his back, Channi stared up at the ceiling. He closed his eyes and counted to six. He would have
counted further, but he could never remember what came
next. He rolled again, three more times, taking himself closer
to the saloon entrance. Turning his head, he squinted under
the gap beneath the doors.

There was man on the opposite side of the street smoking
a cigarette. What an idiot! He must be awful sure of himself,
Channi thought with some humor. Well, this ain't gonna be
his day. "I see him," he hissed.

"Can you shoot him?"

"Not from here."

"Jonas," said Coltrane from out of the gloom. "I'll take Maisie upstairs."

"You'll protect your own skin, you mean!"

"No, no, I swear. I'll—"

"I have a Winchester up there," said Maisie. "We can shoot down into the street from the bedroom window."

"It's too dark."

"Not if we see the flash of their guns," said Coltrane quickly, grabbed Maisie by the hand, and raced to the stairs. He cracked his shins into the occasional chair as he went, but nothing was going to stop him.

Jonas watched them ascend through the gloom. If there was a Winchester, that would give them an edge, so he waited, keeping his breathing even, knowing this wasn't part of his overall plan. Whoever these people were, they were going to pay for coming up against Jonas like this. "Shoot him, Channi!"

"I'm not in range. But without a light, I might just be able to get closer. He won't see me come out."

He sat up and shot to pieces the last remaining oil lamp. Some of the oil caught fire. Cursing, Sefton the barkeep, ran out from behind the counter and, using a couple of bar towels and a glass of frothy beer, quickly stamped down the flames.

A pall of acrid smoke drifted across the still saloon, now plunged in virtual darkness. What little light left coming from the pale grey sky outside proved too weak to filter into the room.

Channi took his chance. Jumping to his feet, he went through the batwing doors, revolver straight ahead of him, and fired off round after round into the figure standing under the porch. After the third shot, the sound of shattering glass rang out through the silence, but he did not cease firing.

Bemused, some half-dozen paces from where he thought he'd seen the figure arrogantly smoking a cigarette, he stopped, ejecting cartridges. A sound behind him caused him to turn.

There, black against the edifice of the saloon, was a tall man in a frock coat, his marshal's badge glinting dully in the gloom, a halo of fluttering snowflakes giving him an almost ghost-like appearance. In his hands he held a scattergun. He eased back the hammers. "Drop the gun."

Gaping, Channi didn't know what to do. He looked back into the porch. Where was the figure? What had happened to him?

Then, he saw it.

The figure.

Positioned slightly opposite to where Channi thought he was, the man stepped down into the street, still smoking. As he came closer, his boots crushed mirrored glass into the frozen ground. He was laughing.

Channi looked from the figure to his empty gun and groaned.

Lost in the darkness, Jonas decided there was only one option left for him – to flee.

Groping across the room, hoping his memory would serve him well, he managed to find the table and the saddlebags. He threw them over his shoulder and, with one hand outstretched and the other holding his gun, he made his way towards the rear. There had to be a back entrance, then it would be a simple case of sprinting to the livery, finding his horse, and making good his escape.

It was going to take some time, and more than once, he lost his way. Struggling to keep the threat of panic well battened down, he found the far wall and shuffled along it inch by painful inch.

Under the stairs, he found a door and went inside.

Small, airless, this had to be the way.

He clattered into a collection of what felt like metal buckets or pots and fell over, sending the saddlebags skidding across the floor. This was no way out and he cursed loudly, almost losing control. He sat and swallowed down his anger and lack of luck, thinking what to do and where to go.

From the bedroom in which they had spent so many tender moments, Maisie reached under the bed and pulled out the Winchester. Coltrane, meanwhile, put a match to the small, bedside oil lamp and sighed in relief as the sickly yellow light drizzled out to give some respite from the all-consuming darkness.

Moving up close, Coltrane placed a hand gently on her shoulder. Keeping his voice low, he said, "We don't have to do this."

"What do you mean?"

He nodded towards the Winchester in her hands. "We don't have to shoot anyone. We can get the money and go like we said. Make it across to California, start a new life. You and me."

"And Jonas? You think he's going to let us do that?"

"We can take the back stairs, and before anyone realizes, we'll be on our way." Sighing, he sat down beside her. "Jonas is not going to give himself up. He'll try and shoot it out. If we're lucky, he'll get himself killed."

"Or he'll kill them – whoever they are."

"By the time the shooting has died down, we'll be long gone." He nodded again at the Winchester. "Are you any good with that thing?"

A tiny laugh. "Better than most. I've had many years of taking good care of myself."

"And have you ever shot anyone with it?"

"Once. A few years ago, cowboy was beating up one of the girls. Bad. Real bad. I took this rifle, leaned over the balcony, and shot him dead."

"Dear God."

"What's the matter? You think because I'm a weak and defenseless woman I'm not capable?"

"Maisie, I believe you are more than capable." He turned his gaze to the window. "How's about you lean over the balcony again, only this time you shoot Jonas?"

"Are you crazy? What if I miss? In the darkness of the barroom, it's more than likely. Then what? He'll be hell-bent on killing us after that."

Rubbing his face, Coltrane stood up and paced the room. "All right, then we have to take the back stairs. If he comes after us, you try and shoot him then. We have little choice. If he survives, we're more than likely be dead, and if he doesn't, we have a fairly even chance of getting out of this alive."

"Those ain't good odds."

"They're all we have."

They stared into one another's eyes and made their decision.

CHAPTER TWENTY-EIGHT

Hearts pounded in constricted chests.

The horror of gunfights. The promise of almost certain death.

It twists minds, seizes muscle, makes life appear momentary, fleeting. No time to wonder what might have been, all those lost dreams, missed opportunities. No time for anything else except thinking about survival.

In any way possible.

Channi tried.

He turned, hoping to wrong-foot the man in front of him. If he could gain some distance, he might be able to reload his gun, shoot, escape.

But his mind was clouded. The instinct to live.

He spun on his heels, and the other one, the one with the scattergun, dealt him a horrific blow across the side of the head with the stock, pitching him to the ground, all senses gone.

He wasn't quite unconscious. Voices came to him,

jumbled up, like tongues. He remembered his old preacher explaining tongues. He never explained how to count, though. Useless old preacher.

Hands were grabbing him, dragging him across the ground, exposed stones biting into his flesh. So hard, so cold. Then they lifted him.

So cold.

The wind rattled through the warped and twisted boards of the crumbling buildings.

He wished he was anywhere else but here. If only he'd made his own way south.

If only.

Channi twisted his neck, tried to focus and recognize the faces of those who were attacking him, wrenching away his future. His life.

A second, heavier blow smashed into his guts, and he thought he would be sick before everything disappeared into an endless black, spiraling hole.

Jonas tried.

Swearing, he managed to find the saddlebags before he clawed the door to the tiny room open and made his way back into the saloon.

"Sefton? Sefton, are you there?"

"Jonas? Is that you? I can't see anything."

"Where are you?"

"Behind the bar, and I ain't coming out – I don't wanna get shot by accident. Who are those men outside?"

"Beats me – bounty hunters or lawmen, it makes no difference – they're out to kill us. Where's the back way to the street?"

"Here, behind the counter. But if you go out there, they'll shoot you dead."

"No. They're too busy with Channi. You have a shotgun behind there, don't you?"

"Yeah, but I'm not that good."

"No need to be."

Jonas groped his way behind the bar. His eyes were much more accustomed to the gloom now and he saw the draped curtain and the promise of a back room. "Is it through this here curtain?"

"Straight ahead. There's back stairs too."

"All right. Put two rounds through the main doors as soon as I shout out to you."

"Hell, Jonas, I don't know if I can—"

"Just do it, Sefton!" and without another word, he went through the curtain.

Maisie tried.

She knew Coltrane's words made sense, but she also knew none of this would end until those pursuing them were dead.

She had plans.

She had dreams.

All her life, she'd done what others wanted. Men mostly. She believed the Doc offered security. She believed him to be rich. He promised her he'd take her away to the better life she'd always wanted.

But he lied.

They all lied.

Stroking the Winchester, she smiled at Coltrane. "I'm gonna make things right. I'm gonna make sure we never have to live in fear again."

She stood up. Coltrane reached out to grab a handful of her skirt, but she tugged herself free, engaged the Winchester, and went to the window.

. . .

Doc Farlow tried.

Tried to get himself out of his bed.

He sat gasping, holding his side, waiting for the waves of pain to die away. They hardly did. From under the pillow, he brought out the old Colt Navy, the only gun he'd ever possessed. The one holstered to his hip during his years as an Army medic during the War. He'd never fired it, but always kept it meticulously clean knowing that one day he would need it.

That day was now.

Steadying himself, he took a breath and stood up, sucking in air as the pain stabbed into his body. Too old for something like this, he chastised himself. Let it go.

But he knew he couldn't and, in a swaying gait, crossed over to the door.

Channi hung in the man's grip. There was nowhere else to go, nothing more to do.

Jonas curled his hand around the door handle. He lifted his head to shout out to Sefton.

Masie raised the window and, kneeling, rested the Winchester barrel on the bottom ledge. The night was black. She saw shapes. She took her aim.

Doc Farlow stepped onto the landing, pausing to gather his strength. Bent over, one hand pressed against the wall, drawing in ragged breaths. He took his time.

Soon. One more effort. Monumental or otherwise, he couldn't live with the shame of it, the ignominy. There was no choice.

Everything came to this.

CHAPTER TWENTY-NINE

From where he was, Roose heard a voice from inside the saloon shouting, "Now, Sefton!" just as a red-hot bullet shot harmlessly above his head. Reacting quickly, he swung Channi in front of him just in time as a second bullet thudded into the bank robber's chest. Holding the stricken man upright and using him as a shield, Roose fired three rounds into the upstairs window from where the shots were fired and, pushing Channi aside, ran to the saloon doors.

Half-a-dozen paces from making it, the doors exploded into a shower of splintered wood causing Roose to hurl himself sideways. Rolling out of harm's way, he glanced up to see Whit going through what remained of the doors. He swore, stood up, and ran after the marshal.

There was a man behind the counter, doing his level best to reload the shotgun. Whit didn't have time for debate and emptied both barrels of his scattergun into him. The spread hit the countertop, sending out a shower of sharp wood splinters straight into the man's body. He was screaming when he went down. Whit broke open his gun and feverishly reloaded.

Coltrane was dragging her from the window. "For pity's sake, Maisie, do you want to get us both killed?"

"I'm all right," she said, knocking away his hand and working the lever. "I got one of 'em. I think the other one has come inside.

A shotgun boomed from below. Then, seconds later, another twin blast. Coltrane glared at her, unable to register what was happening. "We're gonna die, Maisie!"

"Man up," she spat and got to her feet.

The bedroom door burst open.

Farlow stood in the open doorway, breathing hard, face covered in sweat. A maniacal grin split his face. "See you in hell," he said.

Dumbstruck, neither Coltrane nor Maisie had any time to react before Doc Farlow put a fusillade of bullets into both of them.

Jonas staggered outside, the cold night air almost taking his breath away. He wore no coat, but such luxuries were beyond him now. The night pressed in all around him, and for a moment, he struggled to get his bearings. A sudden arc of light brought some relief from the darkness, but only briefly. An oil lamp, pitching through the air, hit the ground and burst open, the oil igniting. Behind the orange glow, Jonas saw the outline of a man.

"This is for Brown Owl," said a voice.

Jonas, not knowing who Brown Owl could be, reacted in the only way he knew how. One of them must have managed to hide out back, waiting to ambush him. Well, that was his mistake. Diving full stretch to his right, Jonas brought up his already drawn six-gun and fanned the hammer.

Unfortunately for Jonas, he had no real idea where his attacker was and the shots went wide and wild. Snorting, he climbed to his feet, snapping his head from side to side. "Where the hell are you?"

Cole, who knew exactly where Jonas was, breathed, "Turn around."

Jonas did so. His hands were shaking, his mouth gaping open, voice trembling with dread, "Who ..."

"You killed my friend. Now, you're gonna pay."

"Friend? Mister, I don't know who you mean but I swear I—"

"The Indian scout. Name of Brown Owl."

The beginning of something, a recall, a realization, stirred from within. One hand came up, "Hey, now wait a moment, I—"

Cole put two bullets into him, the heavy slugs throwing the man backwards. He hit the ground, writhing. Cole stepped closer stepped closer, stared into the terrified dying man's eyes, and put a third round into his head.

Breathing a long sigh, Cole ejected the spent bullets, reloaded and holstered his Colt. He turned away. For a moment he allowed himself a brief memory of his fellow scout, Brown Owl, to invade his thoughts. He muttered, "So long old friend," and went through the back entrance to the saloon.

Behind the curtain, he took the gas lamp that was balanced precariously on a lob-sided preparation table and went into the saloon.

Despite the murkiness, he assessed the situation fairly quickly. He saw Whit snapping his scattergun closed. They exchanged a look. "Is that you, Cole?"

"I hope for your sake it is."

The Marshal laughed and went to take a step forwards. A bullet hit him in the left bicep, spinning him around and finally dropping him to his knees, the scattergun falling from numbed fingers.

Several more bullets slapped into the wooden floor around him. Cole turned and saw a small, huddled figure coming down the stairs one at a time and shot him, throwing him backwards against the steps. His firearm clattered down to the floor. Holding the oil lamp aloft, Cole went and checked on him. The old coot, for he was indeed old, lay with his eyes wide open, stone dead.

Roose came crashing through the broken batwing doors, gun drawn, swiveling his head left and right, trying his best to gain some focus on what was occurring.

"Hold on, Sterling," said Cole, and he laid the oil lamp on the countertop. "We have yet another walking wounded to tend to."

Whit groaned, turned over and sat there, right hand flat against his left arm, blood leaking between his fingers. He looked as if he'd aged ten years.

"Does this mean there ain't gonna be a hanging?" asked Roose.

"Seems like," said Cole and holstered his gun.

"There's the fella we found out on the prairie," said Whit, head down, suffering.

"Ah, good," said Cole, "I wouldn't like the party to have been completely spoiled." Then, shaking his head, he went back around the counter, stepped over the ruined corpse of a man lying there, and brought down a bottle of whisky from the shelf.

"You celebrating?" asked Roose.

"Kind of," said Cole, pulled off his neckerchief and soaked it in whisky. Coming around the counter again, he got down next to Whit and grinned. "This is gonna hurt, Marshal," and he pressed it against the man's shot arm with some considerable relish.

CHAPTER THIRTY

"We can't do that," said Larry Grimes, sitting in the back room of his store with Cathy next to him. "It's immoral!"

"I don't really care what it is anymore, Larry. Neither of us have been dealt a good hand in this life, not until now, that is. So we're gonna use that money, pull down that old house of yours and employ some *real* builders to make us a new home – and a bigger one!"

"But, Cathy, don't you think we should—"

"What? Give it back?" Larry nodded. "Well, no, I do not think we shall. I have thought long and hard on this, Larry, since Mr Norton told me about the money. I was like you, at first, but I think we have just as much right to some happiness as the next person. Besides, it was what Mr Norton wanted."

It was late. Cathy had told him the whole story of what had occurred with Simpson and Cruces, of the killing and how she never wanted to set foot in that cabin again. Larry listened and knew she was not to be deterred. The more he thought, the more he begrudgingly came to agree with her. It was a wonderful plan, and he wholeheartedly agreed.

They spent the night in the local hotel, in separate rooms, and the next morning, over the breakfast table, Larry announced that he had sent off to Kansas City for a diamond ring, to make their engagement official. Cathy burst into tears, but for the first time for as long as she could remember, they were tears of happiness.

Towards mid-afternoon, with Larry once again behind the counter of his store, Cathy received Florence Caitlin's congratulations with much blushing. As they both stood exchanging stories about Larry and his somewhat dubious reputation, Cole and Roose rode into town, with Whit behind them looking ashen-faced. A long line of horses, with bodies draped across their backs, accompanied them. Cathy was already running down the steps as Roose reined in his horse.

"Oh, Mr Roose," she said, "what in the name of heaven happened?"

"Nothing that heaven has got anything to do with. I need to know where your doctor is, Miss Courtauld, so we can get this good man looked after. He's as tough as an old mule, but he's lost a lot of blood."

"I'll show you," said Florence, coming down the steps.

Roose doffed his hat and smiled, "Why thank you, Miss."

"Name is Florence Caitlin, as well you should know, Sheriff."

"He don't have much call to be associating with pretty ladies," said Cole from a few feet away.

"That is the truth," said Roose. "I am somewhat busy, as you might say."

Florence gave him a look and crossed to Cole. "I'll show you where Doc Henson's place is."

"Thank you kindly," said Cole, gave Roose a wink, and guided himself and Whit in the direction Florence took them.

Roose looked down at Cathy and pulled a face, gesturing behind him to the string of horses and their grizzly cargo. He wrinkled his nose. "They is somewhat ripe, Miss Courtauld."

"Ain't they just," she said, pressing a handkerchief against her nose.

"I shall deliver them to the undertaker's, then I shall need to come and talk to you. We have some loose ends to tie up."

She watched him go as Larry came down the steps to join her. "What did he mean by that?"

"I'm not sure."

"The money? He knows about it, don't he! Dear Lord, Cathy, we is gonna end up in deep trouble after this."

"No, we ain't, Larry Grimes, unless you open your big mouth."

"I won't, I swear to you."

"Well, all right then," and she pushed past him and went inside the store.

"So that is it," said Roose sometime later, peering at her from across the table.

"Every detail."

"You shot him?"

"I did. And I'd do it again if I had to."

"*Cathy*!" burst out Larry.

Roose held up his hand. "Don't go getting irate, Larry. What's done is done."

Larry gaped at him. "You mean there won't be any charges?"

Sweeping up his hat, Roose stood up. "Well, from where I'm standing, I can't say much wrong has been done. A case of self-defense is how I'd put it." He adjusted his hat on his head and smiled. "How much do you think that young fella you helped took from the bank?"

Cathy's face fell, and, beside her, Larry yelped.

"Well?"

Cathy and Larry exchanged a glance. Dropping her head and voice, Cathy said, "Ten thousand dollars."

There was a long pause before Roose said, "You've lost a good deal. Things have a way of evening out in life is how I see it." Her face came up, wide-eyed in disbelief. "And, I do believe congratulations are in order?"

Cathy gasped. "How did you know?"

"It's my duty to know, Miss Courtauld."

"Cathy."

He smiled again and left.

It didn't take Roose long to wander down to the bank. Cole was waiting for him outside and handed him the telegram as he came up the steps.

"How's Whit?"

"He'll make it. Jim Riley from the telegraph office delivered that to him."

"You read it."

"Whit asked me to."

Grunting, Roose read through the words and sighed. "As we suspected."

"Lister tried to embezzle the railroad out of twenty-five thousand dollars," said Cole. "Can't blame him for trying."

"The man's a weasel."

"How long will he get?"

Roose shrugged. "Depends on the railroad, but no more than six months. He'll lose his job, though, which is probably more of a punishment."

"Crime never does pay."

Smiling, Roose turned towards Larry Grimes' store and sighed. "Almost never," he said, and with that, he went through the bank door, with Cole close behind, to arrest Mr Lister, the bank manager.

THE END

Dear reader,

We hope you enjoyed reading *No One Can Hide*. Please take a moment to leave a review, even if it's a short one. Your opinion is important to us.

Discover more books by Stuart G. Yates at https://www.nextchapter.pub/authors/stuart-g-yates

Want to know when one of our books is free or discounted? Join the newsletter at http://eepurl.com/bqqB3H

Best regards,

Stuart G. Yates and the Next Chapter Team

You might also like:

Murdered by Crows by Stuart G. Yates

To read the first chapter for free, please head to:
https://www.nextchapter.pub/books/murdered-by-crows

Lightning Source UK Ltd.
Milton Keynes UK
UKHW021849260121
377731UK00009B/658/J